CW01064187

Love, Lies and Pumpkin Spice

A Slice of Life Cozy Mystery, Volume 1

Rachel Beattie

Published by Rachel Beattie, 2024.

This is a work of fiction. Similarities to real people, places, or events are entirely coincidental.

LOVE, LIES AND PUMPKIN SPICE

First edition. September 27, 2024.

ISBN: 979-8227384782

Written by Rachel Beattie.

Chapter One

There's a muffled cough, the mechanical creak of a hospital bed and then I hear it. A thin, reedy voice that mumbles half a dozen words.

"You know, I'm not dead yet."

This comment might have been a bit more reassuring if it hadn't been almost entirely drowned out by the beeps and whirs of a dozen different machines my decidedly unwell - but apparently still living - father is currently hooked up to.

"Ronnie?" He pulls the oxygen mask away from his face and tries again. "I said I'm fine!"

"You're not fine, Dad." I eye the open door to his hospital room and hastily replace his oxygen mask before an officious nurse can come and do it for him. "You had a heart attack."

Myocardial Infarction, according to the doctor I've just spoken to. *He's lucky to be alive.* I draw in a shaky breath and check my watch.

"Mmmf-hmmmf-mmm-buh?"

His oxygen mask is still obediently in place but I can see the twinkle in my dad's eyes which reassures me that he certainly isn't dead yet. I arch an eyebrow and he eases the mask by an inch, just enough for him to speak without every word being indecipherable.

"You got somewhere else to be, sweetheart?" He bats his eyelashes at me on the last word, then obediently replaces his mask before waving me towards the door. *Go right ahead,* the gesture says. *Don't let me keep you.*

"You don't get rid of me that easily." I perch next to him on the bed, then stoop and press a kiss to his forehead. "Now can you at least try to get some rest until Dr. Stephens comes back?"

"Mmmf-hmmf-mmm-buh!"

"Hey!" I swat him lightly on the shoulder and obediently get to my feet. There's no need for him to translate that particular insult. *I would if you weren't taking up so much space.*

"Hey! No beating up the patient on my watch, please!"

As if on cue, Dr. Stephens strolls back into the room with an affable smile on his face. He glares at my dad and I sense him dropping his hand before he even tries to move his mask.

"Mr. Swan, how's that IV treating you?" He rounds the bed and examines the line in Dad's arm, before consulting his chart and making a note of something. "Well, things are looking a lot better than they were this morning! I don't suppose I need to tell you that. Feeling better?" He lifts his gaze just for a moment and smiles as Dad rolls his eyes. "You will be soon, I promise. Ms. Swan?" He turns to me. "Can I have a word?"

I glance at Dad but I can see his eyelids are already starting to droop, and I decide that us stepping out of his room for a minute might be just what he needs to actually sleep. I follow the doctor into the corridor.

"Ms. Swan."

"Veronica." My polite smile falters at the serious note in Dr. Stephen's voice. "How's he doing, really?" I didn't see Dad when they brought him in, but I remember the panic I felt when I got the message that he had been rushed to hospital with a suspected heart attack. If the frail and pale version of my father that's haunting that hospital bed is him *looking a lot better* then I can only imagine how dire things were earlier today. I shiver, thinking of how they might have turned out. *Or might still turn out.* Black spots appear at the edge of my vision and I casually lean one hand on the wall to steady myself. I'm not as good at playing casual as I think. Dr. Stephens steers me toward a bank of chairs lining the corridor.

"How are you?" he asks, frowning at me. "You don't live here in Westhaven do you?"

"Lincoln," I say. "It's not far." *Especially if you take the back roads and ignore all the speed limits.* I think back to my chaotic journey here and thank my lucky stars I didn't pass a police car.

"Hmm." Dr. Stephens is certainly a lot more perceptive than I usually expect doctors to be but maybe that's the difference between an occasional visit to a crowded city ER and a small town hospital like this one.

"I can stay here as long as Dad needs me to," I say, firmly redirecting Dr. Stephens back to the matter at hand. "How is he, really?"

"Well, he had a very serious episode this morning." Dr. Stephens glances over his chart. "And it looks like this wasn't the first attack he's had, although this was a much more serious incident." He pauses. "He's very lucky, Ms. Swan. Next time, he might not be."

Next time? Dr. Stephens must hear my shocked intake of breath because he lifts his gaze and smiles at me.

"But we're going to do everything it takes to make sure there never is a next time." He begins outlining a plan that starts with tests and medication, lifestyle changes, and regular monitoring. "And of course, there's always a surgical option on the table." His lips quirk. "If you'll pardon the pun."

"Surgery." I let out a breath I wasn't even aware I was holding.

"It might be avoidable." Dr. Stephens shrugs his shoulders. "At the moment there is so much we still don't know. So I'm going to suggest - very strongly - that your father makes himself comfortable here at St Joseph's because he's going to be here for a little while."

"Right." I try to smile, but I feel like crying and it's pretty obvious my attempt at cheer isn't the least bit convincing. "Well, we'll do whatever you think is best."

"Of course you will." He pats me gently on the shoulder. "I can see you're a good daughter, Veronica. And your father has a strong will. He's a fighter. That's good."

I pull a face and Dr. Stephens chuckles.

"Trust me. It's a good thing. He's got a lot of reasons to keep living, and number one is sitting right here in front of me. We're going to take good care of your father, and with you here to help we'll soon get him back on his feet."

• • • •

WALKING ALONG THE WESTHAVEN high street is like walking through a memory. It's actually kind of eerie seeing how little has changed in my hometown since I've been gone. *It's only been a few years*, I remind myself. *What were you expecting?* I come to a stop outside the Slice of Life and look up at the retro diner that has been like a second home for me for as long as I can remember. Instead of babysitters, I spent my childhood getting underfoot and eating my body weight in cookie dough. As a teenager, I was either studying in one of the booths here or pulling a waitressing shift to earn my allowance. And not a single thing about it has changed.

"Are you coming or going? Or just blocking the path for fun?"

I turn at the cantankerous, old-man voice and see its owner change from a scowl to a smile.

"Veronica Swan!"

"Mr. Hamilton!" My old English teacher looks a little older and frailer, but he's in the same plaid button-down and faded chinos that I remember from every third-period literature class I took in high school.

"You might as well call me George now," he says, peering down at me from over the top of his wire-rimmed spectacles. "I ain't Mr. Anybody no more." He tucks his thumbs into the waistband of his pants and pulls them up, surveying me with suspicion. "So, which is it? Coming? Or going?" He furrows his brow. "Or just standing between me and my afternoon coffee?"

I laugh and jump to the side, ushering him through the door ahead of me.

"That's more like it," he grumbles, as he shuffles into the diner. "Matthew! Found a stray. Where's my coffee?"

As I cross the threshold of the diner my heart plummets. *Matt is here?* My mind catches up a moment later. Of course Matt is here. Where else would he be at three o'clock on a Tuesday afternoon?

"Coming right up, Mr. Ham - ah - George."

The familiar voice of my oldest friend floods me with such warmth and affection after the emotional turmoil of the past twenty-four hours that I barely have time to process it before he comes into view, his cheerful expression shifting into a grin as he recognizes me.

"No way!"

Before I have time to protest, he vaults over the counter, sliding nimbly past George Hamilton to wrap me in the kind of bear hug I haven't experienced since leaving Westhaven to go to college. It's exactly what I've needed, and I lean into it for all of a moment before we both stiffen and break apart, feeling shy and sheepish at the realization we aren't kids anymore, and we haven't seen each other - or even spoken to each other - in years.

"How's your dad?" Matt asks, taking a step back and beckoning me further into the diner. "I couldn't believe it when I heard what happened. Is he allowed visitors yet?"

I shake my head.

"Not yet. Hopefully in a day or two. They're keeping him in for a little while for observation and while they tinker with his meds. Then home." I smile, wryly. "And a lifestyle overhaul."

"Oh, he is going to love that."

"It's better than the alternative," I say, shaking my head before the worst-case scenario *alternative* can settle for too long in my imagination. "They're threatening him with surgery if we can't make some major changes."

"Oof." Matt glances over his shoulder at a rack of pre-cut cakes and pastries. "I guess I'd better work on some heart-healthy alternatives to all this then, huh?" He winks. "Don't want to lose my best customer."

Mr. Hamilton pointedly clears his throat as he makes his way slowly to a booth and carefully slides in.

"*One of my best* customers."

"That's better." The old man smacks his hand against the tabletop. "Now where's my coffee?"

"Coming right up." Matt shoots me an amused look. "You want a slice of pie to go with that? Or can I persuade you to try my apple pancakes? I'm still tweaking the recipe and could use your expert opinion..."

"I'm assuming those apple pancakes come doused in cinnamon?"

Matt nods.

"Better not, in that case. I'm allergic, and despite having me on pills for just about every other ailment there is they haven't cured that just yet." Mr. Hamilton shimmies in his seat. "So many pills I practically rattle. Trust me, you two, getting old ain't for the weak, that's for sure. Veronica!"

He shifts so quickly into barking my name that I jump.

"Come and sit down. You can tell me everything you've been up to since you left this dead-end town."

Exchanging a glance with Matt I obediently hurry along to Mr. Hamilton's booth and slide in opposite him.

"There's not much to tell," I begin, feeling the sharp scrutiny of his dark eyes from behind his glasses.

"I find that hard to believe. Westhaven High's star pupil gets an academic scholarship to a top college and shoots off like a rocket, never to be seen again."

"Until now." I'm grateful when Matt appears, carrying two cups of coffee that he places silently on the table before winking at me and retreating.

We both grew up with George Hamilton as our English teacher and I'm sure he's been a victim of this kind of inquisition himself before now.

"So how is your dad, really?" Mr. Hamilton asks, after taking a sip of his coffee. "Heart attack, wasn't it?" He thumps his chest. "'Bout the only thing of mine that still works without help is the old ticker." He frowns. "You tell him we're all pulling for him, won't you?"

I'm touched by the affection in the older man's eyes and reassure him that I will.

"'Course I'm pretty sure he just did it to get out of paying his debts."

"What?"

"Gambling debts. Poker." Mr. Hamilton snorts into his coffee. "Don't look so scandalized. We only play for pennies. And bragging rights." He knocks on the surface of the table. "You tell Ed I'm keeping track and we can pick right up where we left off once he's back on his feet."

"Here! I made a fresh batch just for you."

Matt appears at our table again, this time with two plates boasting a freshly made stack of pancakes. The scent of sugared apples makes my mouth water and I eagerly dive in, relishing my first bite and realizing just how long it's been since I ate anything.

"Dig in," Matt encourages Mr. Hamilton, who's warily eyeing his stack. "There's no cinnamon, I promise."

"Well, alright." He takes a dubious bite, then smiles. "Very good." A second and third bite follow swiftly before he lifts his fork in an appreciative salute. "You know, Matthew, you should think about running a diner. You've got the knack."

Matt laughs and retreats to the counter, leaving me and Mr. Hamilton to enjoy our meal in peace.

"So, how's work?" Mr. Hamilton asks after a minute or two. "They ok with you taking some time off?"

"I can work remotely," I say, automatically.

"What about your friends? Boyfriend?"

"They're fine. They understand." This particular line of questioning does a number on my appetite and after a few more bites I push my plate away, half-finished.

"So you're going to be staying in Westhaven for a while?"

"Looks like it." I drum my fingers on the table, wondering how and when I'll be able to extricate myself from Mr. Hamilton's grip. It's not that I don't enjoy catching up with my favorite former teacher, but I can live without his scrutiny. *Maybe if my life wasn't such a disaster* before *I got called home...*

"You'll be here for the pie festival, then."

"The what?"

Mr. Hamilton eyes me over the top of his glasses, then carefully puts down his knife and fork and speaks slowly, as if addressing a very small child.

"The Westhaven Winter Pie Festival. I mean, I guess October isn't exactly *Winter*, but..."

"They still have that?"

"They most certainly do. It's the highlight of the social season for some people." He raises a hand and waves to get Matt's attention, then beckons him back over to join us.

"What's up?" Matt notices my plate. "You didn't like them? Let me make you something else."

"No, no!" I keep hold of my plate and smile at his eagerness to please. "They're great. I'm just not very hungry."

"In that case..." Mr. Hamilton leans across the table and spears one of my untouched pancakes with his fork, adding it to his own pile. When he speaks again, his words are muffled with chewing and I see Matt stifle a laugh. "Matthew, tell Veronica here she ought to take part in the pie festival."

"You ought to take part in the pie festival," Matt repeats automatically, then nods at me. "No, really. You should!"

"Are you entering?"

"I'm not allowed." He lays a hand over his chest. "No professionals permitted." He winks. "But you...."

"Well, I'm the daughter of a professional." I think of my dad, and then remember his cooking skills didn't exactly pass to me. "I'll think about it," I say, privately vowing to avoid both competing and attending the festival. There's nothing like a small-town gathering to get the gossip circling, and if there's one thing I can live without, it's Westhaven's Women's League zeroing in on me and my failure to reach my potential.

"Matthew can't take part, but he could certainly help you out, couldn't you, Matt?" Mr. Hamilton eyes Matt with a mysterious gleam in his dark eyes. "That is if his girlfriend hasn't already got a claim on every free hour he has..."

Girlfriend? I look at Matt but he's already retreating to greet his next customer, who comes flying through the door, filling the diner with a shrill, one-sided argument.

"Well, of course I tried that, Erik. I'm not *stupid*. But -" She seems to notice for the first time that she's in a public place and her whole demeanor shifts. "I'll have to call you back." She ends the call and drops her phone into the kind of designer purse I've only ever seen knock-off versions of up close. I turn away but not quickly enough.

"Veronica? Is that you?" Heels clatter noisily on the diner's worn parquet floor as my former high-school nemesis stalks towards us and I see Mr. Hamilton settle comfortably into his side of the booth to watch our reunion with amusement. "It is! I can't believe it!" She leans down and drops a noisy air kiss somewhere in the vicinity of my cheek. "Veronica Swan!"

"Bella Duke." I try and fail to inject my voice with enthusiasm.

"Not Duke." Bella shakes her head and then shoves her left hand into my face, almost taking my eye out with the huge rock that adorns her ring finger, alongside a matching wedding band. "Bella *Villodan* now."

"Oh." I smile. "Well, congratulations." I sift through my memories for why that last name sounds familiar. "Wait, *Villodan* like *Erik Villodan*?"

"That's right." Bella nods smugly. "We've been married two years now."

"Congratulations," I say again, biting my lip to keep from asking what happened to Erik's first wife. Christina had been a couple of years older than us at school like Erik was, but they'd been the golden couple for years and got married right after graduation. They always seemed so perfect together but I guess appearances can be deceptive.

"So what are you doing here?" Bella bumps me along the booth and slides in next to me, not giving me a chance to protest. "I thought you were some high-flying...something..." She looks at me, her smile faltering into a barely constrained grimace and I self-consciously brush a lock of loose hair behind one ear, hastily buttoning up the faded knit cardigan I pulled on at stupid-o'clock this morning when I first got the call to come home. I haven't even looked in a mirror and dread to think what I look like next to prim, perfect Bella Duke. *Bella Villodan*. That's going to take some getting used to.

"My dad," I begin.

"Oh, yes of course!" Bella's voice drips with faux concern. "I heard all about it. A heart attack, wasn't it? Well, how lovely that he could hang on long enough for you to come home and say your goodbyes."

"He's going to be just fine," I say, frostily. "But your concern is appreciated. I'll tell him you said hello."

"Oh!" Bella giggles awkwardly and slides back out of the booth. "Of course. Well, if you need anything, anything at all, you know exactly where to find me!" She glances dismissively in Mr. Hamilton's direction then turns to find Matt and order her coffee. If I didn't know him better, I'd say he was hiding, but then he appears out of nowhere, clutching a refillable cup that boasts an elegant diamante *B* and holds it out to Bella.

"Your usual," he says, then hovers in place for a moment.

"Thank you, Matthew, darling! Now, about this evening. I told Erik we'd meet you and -"

"Yep, great!" Matt cuts her off and turns abruptly to me. "Did Veronica tell you she's planning to enter this year's Pie Festival?"

"Really?"

I was all set to deny this allegation, but something in Bella's snort of amusement sets my teeth on edge. She is still the same mean girl I remember from high school, only with a cash injection and a new husband to prop up her power stance.

"I'm thinking about it," I say, tilting my chin to look her in the eye. "It's been a while since I baked anything, but -"

"Well, it's an open competition," Bella says, with a disdainful sniff. "Even to amateurs." Her phone starts buzzing noisily in her purse and she reaches for it, glancing warily at me and Mr. Hamilton before accepting the call and hurrying away without another word.

"If I didn't know better, Veronica, I'd take that as a challenge."

I glance at Mr. Hamilton and see his dark eyes twinkling behind his glasses. *I don't have the energy for challenges right now, but if it means knocking Bella off her perch at last, then maybe I can make an exception...*

Chapter Two

In some ways, it's like nothing has changed at home, either. Sure, the yard is looking more than a little overgrown, the porch needs a fresh coat of paint and there's a stack of unread mail, unpaid bills, and old newspapers piled high just inside the door, but home is still *home*. I step carefully over the threshold and draw a breath, then grimace. It doesn't take me long to find the source of the smell. Old pizza, stale and greasy, along with dirty dishes lining just about every available surface of the kitchen. I survey the place, taking in one domestic disaster after another. *It's a good job I came home when I did*, I think, wrinkling my nose as I open the empty refrigerator. *If the heart attack hadn't got Dad, then e coli would!*

"Well," I declare to the empty house. "I do need to keep busy!"

I start with the kitchen, stacking and rinsing plates before loading the dishwasher. I can't find any evidence of cleaning supplies, and that brings my impromptu session to a sudden stop. I whip out my phone, open up the notes section, and start composing a shopping list. *Clorox. Lots of it.* I trace a path through the kitchen into the living room and run a finger along the mantelpiece. *Furniture polish. Garbage bags...* I open the door to the dining room and abruptly back out, closing it again. The dining table is drowning under piles of paperwork and I realise Dad hasn't been coping for a while. *More than a while*, I think as I pass a stack of bills marked *urgent* that haven't even been opened yet. I frown, wondering just when my confident, capable father stopped managing to run his own

14

household. It's not like he hadn't had practice! After losing Mom when I was still in elementary school, the Swan household had functioned pretty well just the two of us, with the occasional visit of my grandmother or my aunt whenever life got especially hectic at the diner. But I guess things have changed here in all sorts of ways I didn't notice at first.

Snatching up my car keys I head straight for the door, planning on a quick dash into town before returning and setting to on the house. I haven't even ventured upstairs yet, but I'm willing to bet there will be plenty to do before I can even think of turning in for the night. I stifle a yawn and pull the front door open, then reel back in surprise to find a woman standing on my front porch with her hand raised as if about to knock.

"Oh!" A brassy laugh sounds and the woman totters backwards. "That can't be Veronica, can it?"

"It most certainly can," I will myself to smile. "Good afternoon, Mrs. Kaufman." I'd recognize that laugh anywhere. And that hairstyle, which I don't think she's changed in the last twenty years. "How can I help you?"

"Actually, I'm here to help you, dear." It's then that I realize Mrs. Pamela Kaufman hasn't come empty-handed. She shoves a covered casserole dish in my direction and waits expectantly for me to take it, which, after a moment's hesitation, I do.

"Thank you?" I can't stop my voice from rising at the end of my sentence, turning my words into a question.

"You're welcome, dear." Mrs. Kaufman looks at me, then leans in, frowning. "How is your poor father?"

"Oh!" Truth dawns on me and I hug the pie dish a little closer. The Westhaven Prayer Chain must have been working overtime. *And I dread to think what the rumor mill has been up to!* "He's - he's doing ok, thank you." I smile or try to. "It's going to be quite a long road from here, I think. He'll be staying in the hospital for now."

"That poor man!" Mrs. Kaufman clucks her tongue. "But at least you'll be here to look after things when he comes home, now, won't you? I always think it's a shame for these poor older gentlemen, widowers, and bachelors, you know, well, it's just not right, is it? They live alone, they never see other people, and well, you can't tell me a man is really capable of keeping house without a woman there to run around after him." She beams at me, and I feel my inner feminist firing up to set Pamela Kaufman straight on a few things, like the fact that we are living in the actual 21st century and men are just as capable as women of keeping a house clean and tidy. Then I recall the chaos I'm leaving behind me and I slip carefully out of the house, letting the front door swing closed behind me. The last thing I need is for her to realize just how badly my father has been managing without me here. Guilt gnaws at me and I shift my hold on the heavy casserole dish.

"Well, at least you won't have to worry about cooking tonight!" Pamela says. "You enjoy that pot roast, dear, and I'll be back tomorrow with something else. You eat normal food, still, don't you?"

"I -"

"I know a lot of you young people get all sorts of ideas when you move to the city." She purses her lips. "My Julia came home from college for the summer and declared she was a vegan. 'Course that only lasted long enough for us to take her down to the ice cream parlor on Seventh and Main, but you know -"

"This is very kind of you, Mrs. Kaufman," I interject, wondering if I'll ever make it off my porch and on with the rest of my jobs before Pamela Kaufman tells me another long and meandering story about her high-achieving daughter. I'm trying to think of a way to delicately extract myself from her story when the shrill beep of a car horn interrupts us and we both turn to see a close-cut grey bobbed head bent over the steering wheel of an old minivan.

"Goodness! There's that Jennifer Gould not giving me five minutes to pass the time of day! Wave, Veronica, dear, so she can see I'm not just standing around chattering without a purpose."

I clumsily shift my hold on the casserole dish, only narrowly avoiding dropping it as I free one hand to wave.

"I supposed I'd better go," she says, with a regretful glance my way. "Your house was the first on our list, but there are quite a few different townsfolk we have to deliver to today." She drops her voice to a whisper. "Older folk, you know. Alone. Infirm. Without family."

Without family? I prickle and can feel my cheeks start to burn. *What am I? Chopped liver?*

"Now you feel free to sing out if you need anything while you're in town, won't you, dear?" Mrs. Kaufman seems entirely oblivious to any slight as she bustles back down the path toward her friend. "And you tell your father we townswomen haven't forgotten him!" Her eyes sparkle as she turns back to me. "We like to do our bit to make sure these old dears don't feel entirely forgotten by the world!"

Old dears? Forgotten by the world? My embarrassment turns to amusement and I manage to hold in a snicker until Pamela and Jennifer drive away. My father is a lot of things, but even laid up in the hospital I can't conceive of him being *old*. And *forgotten*? He owns the most popular diner in all of Westhaven. Without Eddie Swan, there'd be no Slice of Life diner, and without the Slice, Westhaven would be a very different place indeed.

. . . .

A QUICK DASH TO THE store and I'm soon home again to clean before I give my baking muscles a workout. The trouble is, it turns out I don't really have *baking muscles*.

I look around the chaotic kitchen, battling a heavy weight of disappointment. All the effort I made to clean and tidy the place has been undone by my evening's attempts at baking, and I still don't have a pie worth eating. I sniff, and somewhere buried beneath the cinnamon, sugar, and flour that coat every available surface I smell something burning.

"Oh no!"

Oh yes. I yank open the stove door and choke in a cloud of black smoke that billows out into the kitchen. Using the edge of a dish towel I grip the pie dish and lift it out, wincing as the edge of my thumb catches the red-hot rim of the dish. I drop it unhappily onto the stove-top, next to its cousins, and survey the evening's three dismal attempts at pumpkin pie. The first looks pretty near perfect, except for the slice I cut to try - and discarded as soon as I discovered something had gone very wrong indeed with my efforts. For my second pie, I followed the recipe exactly, double and triple-checking every ingredient before it went into the bowl. It's still raw in the middle, despite the edges burning to a crisp. This third effort is burned all the way through, I reckon, and I don't plan to even attempt to chisel it out of the pan to eat.

So much for teaching Bella a lesson. The only thing that's going to come out of my entry to the Winter Pie Contest is going to be humiliation. *That's if I don't manage to poison one of the judges with my appalling attempts at baking!*

I grab a dishcloth and start wiping up the worst of the cinnamon-coated countertop but before I clean more than a couple of inches there's a knock at the door.

If that's Pamela Kaufman come to bring me another meal and poke around for gossip about Dad, so help me...

I toss the dishcloth aside and hurry to answer the door, surprised to find a familiar figure on the other side.

"Matt!"

"I come bearing gifts." Matt thrusts a bag at me and I look down at it, nodding when I see the wrapped leftovers from the diner's day. "Some of the pastries will be going stale by now, but everything's still edible." He hesitates. "Or I could make you something fresh?" The scent of burned sugar and cinnamon reaches his nostrils and he pushes the door open, striding past me into the house without waiting for an invitation. "Ronnie. What have you been doing?"

"Baking!" I hurry after him, pausing to put the bag of baked goods down on the coffee table in the living room as Matt strides straight into the kitchen. "It's a bit of a mess..."

"A bit?" Matt laughs, then goes to examine my pies with a grimace. "Are any of these edible?"

"Not particularly."

He grabs a fork and digs into one, then spits out his mouthful without swallowing.

"What did you do to this pie?"

"I'm not quite sure." I bite my thumbnail. "But I have a feeling that what I thought was sugar...wasn't sugar."

"Salt." Matt looks for a clean glass and fills it from the faucet, draining the whole eight ounces before turning to look at me. "And you know the cinnamon is supposed to go into the pie filling, not onto every available surface you have." He nods at me. "And the chef."

I brush my cheek, mortified at the layer of dust that comes away on my hand.

"You were serious this afternoon about entering the pie contest, then?" He leans one hip against the counter and surveys me with amusement. "Since when does Bella Villodan's opinion matter to you?"

"It doesn't!" I go back to cleaning, grateful for something to distract me from looking at Matt's warm brown eyes. "I just thought it'd be good to do something community-minded while I'm back in town. Something to keep me busy and distracted while Dad's in the hospital."

"Ah."

Matt's phone pings with a notification and when I risk a glance at him he's hastily tapping out a response to it. He catches my eye and straightens, sliding his phone back into his pocket.

"Well then. It's a good job I'm here to help you, isn't it?" He yanks open the dishwasher and begins stacking it with all the dishes I've made a mess of in my abortive baking attempts and I watch, too stunned to respond at first. "We need to clear the decks a bit before we can get started," he says, nodding at the dripping dishcloth uselessly clutched in my hand. "You clean the countertops, I'll wash the dishes. We can have something to eat and then, once the dishwasher is done, I'll show you how to make the kind of pumpkin pie that will make Bella Villodan eat her words." He grins.

My heart lifts. This is certainly a better option than how I had been spending my evening. With two of us on the task, we soon restore order to the kitchen, and then flop down on the sofa while we wait for the dishwasher to finish its cycle. I dig through the bag of food Matt brought and find there's enough to stretch for several meals if I'm careful.

"Oh, and Pamela Kaufman dropped off a casserole, too." I think of the dish sitting patiently in the refrigerator, then look back at the stuffed Tupperware boxes Matt brought with him. "Is that red beans and rice?"

"Of course." Matt hands me the dish and a plastic fork. "You don't think I'd forget to bring your favorite dish with me, do you?"

I smile and dig in, as Matt leans back on the sofa, puts his feet up on the coffee table, and grabs the TV remote. It's almost like old times. Almost...

Ping!

Ping ping ping!

I watch out of the corner of my eye as Matt wriggles around to locate his phone, and then scrolls through his messages. He's halfway through typing a reply when another comes in.

Ping!

Ping ping!

"Someone's popular," I say, taking another bite of my meal.

"Yeah, sorry about that." Matt smiles as he focuses on his phone, tapping it a few times before sliding it away. He looks at me and frowns. "Eat up! I saved that especially for you. Had to fight off at least three Westhaven regulars to make sure there was enough."

"I'm honored."

"You should be." He winks at me then turns back to the TV and his own meal, shoveling in fork after forkful as he catches up with the football scores.

"How is the diner doing, really?" My voice sounds quiet even to my own ears and when Matt doesn't immediately answer I wonder if he hasn't heard me. "I mean, I can help out in whatever way you need while I'm here. I know with Dad being in hospital you're kind of left to run things on your own, and -"

Matt switches off the TV and then turns to look at me, his features pinched with concern.

"Ronnie, I've been running the diner on my own for years. Edgar signed the whole thing over to me months and months ago. Didn't he tell you?"

The flavored rice turns to ash in my mouth and it takes me an effort to chew and swallow without choking. Matt is watching me carefully and I'm still struggling to make sense of his words.

"What?"

"Your dad sold me the diner outright. The Slice of Life is mine."

Chapter Three

I hurry into the hospital on the very edge of visiting hours, scooting past the judgmental eyes of more than one nurse as I slide into my dad's room just before the clock ticks over.

"They'll throw you out in a minute."

Dad's voice is sleepy, but when I look his way he's smiling, which makes me smile too. I cross the room and hug him, amazed at the difference in just the last few hours.

"No oxygen mask?"

"They said I didn't need it." He brushes an imaginary piece of lint off his shoulder, like being elevated to just room air is some great personal achievement. "I told you. I'll be home again in no time."

"I'm sure you will." I settle into the chair next to his bed and stifle a yawn. I spent all of today running around trying to organize things for when Dad comes home - as well as putting in a ton of extra hours at work. I wince, recalling the less-than-sympathetic video call I had with my boss about my messy work schedule and the stark reminder that I'm not exactly irreplaceable.

And that was all around baking the perfect pumpkin pie, thanks to all the tips Matt gave me last night. I was determined to make my entry entirely by myself, but I certainly wouldn't have been as successful without his advice. And of course, my baking efforts today led to yet more chaos in the kitchen. I managed to make a dent in the worst of the mess, but there'll be plenty to do before I get to go to sleep tonight. The thought makes me yawn again and I turn my head, hoping Dad doesn't notice. *No chance.*

"Tired?"

"We didn't all get to spend today in bed," I tease him. "After work, I ducked into the Slice of Life to check on things. Matt is doing a good job of keeping things ticking over, you'll be pleased to know. And I can pitch in while I'm in town, too. So you don't need to worry about the business."

Dad nods, but his smile doesn't quite reach his eyes. I watch him carefully, holding my breath to see if he'll take this opportunity to tell me what Matt already confided. *Oh, by the way, sweetheart, we don't own our family business anymore. I probably should have mentioned that, huh?*

"There's no rush for you to get back on your feet," I say, willing him to tell me the truth. "I'm sure Matt and I can manage between the two of us." I feel my cheeks heat as I say this and make a show of tugging my hair out of its messy ponytail and plaiting it. This buys me a second or two to get my features back under control and when I risk a glance at my dad I see his gaze is averted. If I didn't know better, I'd think he looked...guilty. *As he should! I don't care about him selling the business, but I can't believe he never even told me!* My stomach turns over as I think of everything else my dad has neglected to mention lately. *Like maybe the fact that Matt is in a relationship. I was going to find that out sooner or later, but it would have been good to have a heads-up!*

I shouldn't mind, and I don't. Not really. Matt and I may have grown up together but we hadn't been close in a long time. I just thought I still knew what was going on in his life.

"So, about the diner -"

"You don't need to worry about that, sweetheart." Dad reaches for my hand and squeezes. "Matt can handle everything just fine."

I open my mouth to protest but something in Dad's gaze stops me in my tracks. He doesn't know that Matt told me the truth about the diner, but he's certainly not about to tell me himself now. And if I don't want to get into an argument, I'm going to have to let it go. For now, at least.

Fine. I arrange my features into a smile, reminding myself that my dad is in a hospital bed recovering from a heart attack and now is probably not the time to rake over his business affairs.

"I made a start on cleaning the house." I cringe, thinking about my feminist foremothers banging their heads against the kitchen sinks they spent their lives chained to and carry on, regardless. "There's still some more work to do, but everything will be sorted before you come home."

"Sorted?" Dad bristles. "It was fine just the way it was."

"Right." I frown, wondering if he has any idea what chaos he's been living in for the past however long. "Well, anyway, we'll need to rearrange a few things for when the doctors discharge you."

"How so?"

Jeez, this father of mine is suspicious!

"You might have to sleep downstairs for a little while," I tell him, saving the suggestions for a regular visiting nurse and an exercise program and various other steps Dr. Stephens outlined for another day.

"I can climb a flight of stairs," Dad grumbles. "You don't need to change a thing. I've managed just fine until now, I -"

"And Mrs. Kaufman stopped by with a casserole," I put in, stopping him before he can get in full Edgar Swan flow. I hear one of the machines next to him start to beep insistently and worry about his blood pressure.

"Pamela Kaufman?"

"Do you know any other?" I roll my eyes, then notice the hint of a smile on my father's face and fight the urge to recoil. *My father and...Pamela Kaufman?!* Time to change the subject again, and fast! "And I ran into Mr. Hamilton yesterday. He asked to be remembered to you."

Now it's Dad's turn to roll his eyes.

"He still talking about being escorted off high school property in disgrace?" He sniffs. "Or that ridiculous feud he's caught up in with those neighbors of his?"

"He said not to worry about the gambling debts." I lift my eyebrows and feel the tiniest glimmer of satisfaction at the way Dad hunches down into his pillows, his features pinched and blushing. "Poker, Pa? Really?"

"It was barely even poker," he protests. "Just a chance to sit around and shoot the shi - ah, breeze." He grins and I reach into my purse for the handful of papers I scraped together that looked the most urgently in need of a response.

"I'm sure you won't mind me taking care of these while you're laid up in here, then? You know, when the bills start coming with red *final warning* notices stamped right there on the envelope that means you actually have to do something about them."

"I meant to get to them..." He tugs uncomfortably on the neck of his hospital gown. "If we tell 'em I've just had a heart attack do you think they'll give us an extension? Maybe waive them altogether?"

"You're not very well acquainted with the IRS, are you, Pops?" I laugh and lean forward to brush his thinning grey hair out of his eyes. I press my forehead against his and drop my voice to a whisper. "You had me worried, you know. Don't do that again!"

"Got you to come home for a visit, though, didn't it?" He winks at me then grows serious. "I'll be alright, kiddo. Don't worry. It's going to take a lot more than some dumb ol' heart attack to keep Edgar Swan off the floor."

"It better. Now you settle in and get some more sleep. Your nurse is going to come and turf me out of here any minute now." I hear the slap-slap-slap of sensible shoes on linoleum and get reluctantly to my feet. "I'll be back in the morning, ok? I'm going to stop in on my way to the pie festival." I wink. "And then again in the afternoon, with my winners' ribbon. They said you might even be able to go home if everything keeps trending upwards. But only if you rest, so you can get a jump on that now, alright? Take care."

"You too, Ronnie." He's yawning now and I can see the very moment sleep sweeps over him like a blanket. I creep towards the doorway and slip through it just in time to see a nurse shoo me off the ward, and I walk towards my car, exhausted but a lot more confident about Dad's recovery than I have been.

• • • •

"RONNIE?" I'M HALFWAY towards my car when a familiar voice stops me in my tracks. This isn't the shrill,

Bella-Duke-Villodan screech that makes my skin crawl. This is an older, huskier version of a voice I know only too well.

"TJ?" I turn around, startled to see my old high school friend looking a lot different from the last time I saw him. Instead of ripped denim and faded cotton, he's in an actual white coat, looking so smart and clean-cut that I almost don't recognize him. The hint of stubble and the tiniest glimpse of a tattoo poking out from beneath his sleeves are all the confirmation I need that this is, indeed, my old school friend. "Wow, look at you!"

"Quite the glow up, right?" He laughs, then holds his hands out to me in an awkward half-hug I am only too grateful to accept. "Are you ok?"

I draw in a shaky breath and smile, but I guess it's not all that convincing. TJ slings an arm around my shoulders and turns me back towards the hospital.

"Come on. I'll show you where the good snacks are."

"You...work here?" I still can't quite make the picture I'm seeing fit with my memories of teen-rebel TJ.

"I'm a pharmacist." He grins and I can't help but laugh until he starts to look a little offended. "Hey, it isn't that funny! Let's just say I made good use of my misspent youth." He waves at a couple of staff members as we make our way back through the waiting room and I start to feel a glimmer of newfound respect for my old friend. We pass a couple of different doors and TJ pauses to peer through the windows of a room or two until he finds a space and claims it for us to use. "Sit." He points me towards a chair. "I'll be right back."

He disappears, leaving the heavy hospital door to swing closed behind him and I look around the empty room feeling conspicuously out of place. I shouldn't be here, and I'm about to make a break for it when TJ comes back, with two candy bars in his hands.

"Alrighty, I might have lied about the good snacks. But I did swipe these from the nurses' station, so we'd better eat them quickly before anyone notices they're gone. Peanut crunch or fudge mallow?"

I pick one and he drags a chair over to sit next to me. We eat our candy bars in silence for a minute before TJ starts talking.

"So you're back in Westhaven." His eyes narrow. "Why? I thought when you kicked the dust of this one-horse town off your feet that was it for you. Driving off into the sunset, no turning back."

"That was the plan." I sigh. Of all the people I've seen since coming back to Westhaven, TJ is probably just about the only one I can be totally honest with. He won't judge me if he hears my hot-shot career is little more than typing line after line of detailed but dull analysis - and now even that's rapidly becoming obsolete. He certainly won't judge me for falling out with my roommate, and if I tell him about my last bad breakup he's liable to go driving off to find the guy and knock some sense into him with his own two fists. I sigh and decide all that can wait. It wasn't any of my problems that brought me back to Westhaven, after all. "My dad had a heart attack."

"What?" He looks up, his mouth full of chocolate, and it takes him a moment of hasty chewing and swallowing before he can speak again. "Oh, Ronnie, I'm sorry. Is he going to be ok?"

"I think so." I nod, slowly. "It's going to take some time though. So while he's recuperating I'm going to be in town looking after him. It'll be ages before he's well enough to go back to work, so I guess you're going to see me working back at the Slice again, just like old times." I grin and am surprised when TJ's answering smile is a little hesitant. "What? I'm not above making the odd coffee while I'm in town." He doesn't say anything and I nudge his foot lightly with mine. "We can't all be fancy, white-coat-wearing pharmacists, you know..."

"Hello? Does anybody *work* in this hospital?"

A shrill voice in the corridor makes both our heads swivel towards it and I feel my features fall in a mirror of TJ's. *No way. I can't be this unlucky.* I thought I already had my high school frenemy run-in for the day under my belt, and I did. My Bella Duke run-in. *Bella Villodan.* This voice doesn't belong to Bella Duke-Villodan. It belongs to her high-school bestie, the second of their trifecta of mean girls who terrorized my teenage years. *Anna Chambers. The head of the hydra herself.*

"I guess some things in Westhaven have stayed exactly the way I remember," I say, as TJ gets wearily to his feet and sticks his head out into the corridor. *I was going to have to cross paths with the queen of mean at some point in my time here,* I think, brushing the last of my candy crumbs off my lap and following TJ. *I guess there's no time like the present.*

Anna Chambers's blonde hair is piled on top of her head in a just-the-right-kind-of-tousled up-do, and her irritated expression melts into a smile when she sees TJ and me walking down the corridor towards her.

"Veronica! And TJ." She turns, then realizes her companion has drifted a little away from her. One superior snap of her fingers brings Caroline Mackie - the third of the Wicked Witches of Westhaven - scurrying to her side. "We wanted to hand out a few fliers."

"For the pie festival!" Caroline tosses her head, sending her blond beach waves back over one thin shoulder. She holds out a flier and TJ takes it, looking around for someone to hand it off to.

"Uh, thanks." He passes it to me, then shrugs. "But this is a hospital."

"What, sick people don't like pie?" Caroline beams, then glances at her friend, her smile fading. "I guess sick people *don't* like pie..."

"Not everyone here is sick," I say, wondering why I feel an absurd urge to stand up for Caroline Mackie. She's not exactly the sweet little girl next door she pretended to be in high school, but her malice was always a bit more unintentional than her friends'. Anna Chambers is still looking my way, her eyes narrowed in suspicion.

"You certainly look well, Veronica."

I look at the flier for one more beat before lifting my head and meeting Anna's insincere compliment with an insincere smile. I know I'm a mess. Fortunately, after ten years away from high school, Anna's opinion isn't quite as crushing as it once was.

"I'm running on fumes," I say, with a smile, as I glance at TJ. "My dad is sick."

"How awful!"

Everything about Anna's comment is perfectly on point, but there is zero compassion in her features, and her eyes continue to stay fixed on me without even a flicker.

"He's going to be ok though, isn't he, Ronnie?" TJ comes to my rescue, stopping just short of putting an arm around me. I take comfort from his words and nod.

"He's going to be fine. Eventually." I pass the festival flier back to Caroline, who takes it and sighs, looking around for somewhere to dump the pile she's holding.

"So is there anywhere we can leave these?" She stifles a yawn. "We want to make sure the whole of Westhaven knows about the festival."

"The same festival they have every year at about this time?" TJ's voice rings with gentle teasing.

"This is the first year I've been in charge of the committee." Anna is all business, and suddenly a few things about Westhaven start falling into place for me. Of course Anna Chambers is running the festival committee. She's no longer queen of Westhaven High so she's determined to be queen of Westhaven proper. I watch as she smiles and waves to various townsfolk milling around the waiting area and realize that she's pretty close to achieving her goal. The same glimmer of annoyance I felt meeting Bella Duke-Villodan earlier sparks back to life inside me and I turn back to Caroline with a smile.

"I already have my entry ready to go."

"You're entering?" Her eyes widen in shock and I begin to rethink my sympathy for her. She's just as awful as her friends.

"Yes." *What's more, I'm going to win.*

"What are you baking?"

This question comes from TJ, and he's just as incredulous as Caroline. I shoot him a look and he stammers out a compliment.

"I'm sure whatever it is, it'll be delicious." He grins, then rubs his midsection. "Can't wait to get myself a slice! Tomorrow's going to be a good day. You'll be making your usual, won't you, Anna? Cherry Pie?"

"That's right." Anna gives TJ an arch look as if suspecting him of mockery, but he meets her gaze innocently enough. She clicks her fingers again, summoning Caroline to her side. "Come on, let's get out of here. It's too late to put out any more fliers now." They walk away, pausing after a few steps when Anna turns back to me with a syrupy smile. "See you tomorrow, pumpkin!"

I frown, then realize Anna is referencing my pie. *How does she know I'm making pumpkin pie?* My confidence falters, just a fraction. *Because knowledge is power, and if there's one thing Anna Chambers has always had in this town, it's power.* I guess it won't be as easy as I thought to strike a blow for democracy around here. But that doesn't mean I'm not going to try.

Chapter Four

My pumpkin pie is a thing of beauty. Even in the middle of a table dominated by other entries, I think it stands just a little bit taller and shines just a little bit brighter.

And then Anna Chambers arrives.

"Oh, doesn't everything look so lovely!" Her voice is too bright, her smile too wide, and as her gaze locks on mine I know *lovely* isn't really what she's thinking when she surveys the town's efforts at pie-making. "I don't suppose there's even any space for my humble effort!"

That's when I notice she hasn't arrived alone.

"Matt?"

"Hey, Ronnie." He looks away from me almost straight away, his fleeting smile lasting only a moment. He's holding an elegant, ornamental pie dish, an antique if I'm not mistaken, and it might as well be priceless from the careful way he's holding it.

"I thought professionals weren't allowed to take part in the contest?" I hear the frostiness in my voice and try to soften it with a smile. "Or is this in another unofficial capacity?"

"What's that, babe?"

Matt shakes his head at me, almost imperceptibly, and that's when I realize two things at once. First, that his offer to secretly help me out with my pumpkin pie has to stay just that - a secret - and second, *babe*, Matt's secret girlfriend that nobody thought to warn me about is none other than my high-school frenemy, Anna Chambers. I stare just a moment too long as she slides one perfectly toned arm around Matt's shoulders and leans her head against him.

"I'll find some space for this," Matt says, slipping out of her grasp and approaching the table. Her two friends hurry forward and start clearing pies left and right, creating a central circle just big enough to house Anna's cherry pie which - and I hate to admit this - looks delicious. Even my pumpkin pie, which I'd been so proud of a few minutes ago, pales in comparison to such perfection.

"Alright, alright! There are too many of you in here. This tent is supposed to be for judges only! So everyone who doesn't hold the power of the blue ribbon, scoot!"

Mr. Hamilton shoos the crowd of assembled Westhaven residents outside, and I take one last wistful look at my pie, lost in a crowd of competitors, before stepping out of the tent.

"I still don't think it's fair that he's on the judging committee!"

It takes me a moment to place this whisper as coming from Bella Villodan. My attention was still so hung up on Anna Chambers and Matt – *Anna Chambers and Matt!?* - that I almost missed the other two witches of Westhaven walking right by me.

"He's going to mark my entry down, I just know it. On account of us being neighbors!"

"Well, you have made his life pretty difficult over that boundary line. Erik shouldn't have been so forceful about it all."

"He's made *our* life miserable!" Bella sniffs and I'm hardly surprised when I see her use the corner of her sleeve to dab at her suspiciously dry eyes. *Never one to miss an opportunity for drama.* "You don't know how dreadful it is to deal with him living right next door!"

Something about Bella's words tugs at my memory, and then I recall Dad mentioning something about Mr. Hamilton having a running feud with his neighbors. *Well, if his neighbors are the Villodans, I can kind of understand it.* Poor Mr. Hamilton! I feel another wave of sympathy for him and catch a gleam in Caroline's eyes which suggests she, too, is not entirely on her friend's side.

"Ronnie! There you are." TJ strolls over to me, holding two cups of steaming apple cider. He thrusts one in my direction. "Dropped your pie off ok?"

"I did." I sniff the cider, then take a suspicious sip. I'm instantly transported back to childhood, and greedily down half the cup in one gulp.

"Woah, there. You know this isn't the real stuff." TJ takes a sip of his own drink and winks. "Reckon we could liven today up a little if it was."

"You mean you don't love community events like this?" I nudge him in the ribs. "Where's that good old-fashioned Westhaven Spirit?"

TJ snorts, choking a little on his drink, which just makes me smile wider. My friend looks a lot more like his old self today, in jeans and a faded band t-shirt, his hair a little too long and his eyes bright with amusement. I have missed him. I didn't realize how much.

"Come on," he says, once he can breathe again. "Let's walk the perimeter. They won't announce the winners of the pie contest for ages yet."

I'm reluctant to go too far, but then I catch sight of Anna hanging onto Matt like he's a life-preserver and all at once I want nothing more than to put distance between us. A lot of distance.

"Hey!" TJ jogs a couple of paces to keep up with me. "Are you trying to circle the park in record time or something?"

"Or something," I say shortly, but obediently slow my pace to match the dawdling crowds. I nurse my spiced cider and look at the booths local artisans and small businesses have set up to catch the eye of unsuspecting shoppers. Wherever there's a crowd in Westhaven, there'll be someone trying to sell their wares. The peaceful tinkle of wind-chimes attracts me and I drift towards a stall that's laden with the things. Large, wooden chimes that knock together, and small, silvery ones that make me think of fairy spells. There are sun-catchers too and I'm just admiring a pretty stained-glass sunset when the owner greets me.

"You have a good eye! These sun-catchers are on offer. Two for the price of one." She names a figure and I abruptly let go of the item I was touching. It's not expensive, especially not when I consider the work that's gone into making it, but it's out of my budget at the moment. "Feel free to keep browsing!" The store owner says, apparently sensing that her presence has intimidated me. "I'll be right over here if you have any questions."

I nod, lifting my gaze just long enough to catch sight of her long, greying hair tied in an elaborate series of braids. I squint. *Prematurely* greying, surely? This woman isn't that much older than I am.

"Ms. Barnes?"

A sparkling laugh confirms my guess is correct.

"Goodness, I haven't heard that name in...five years! It's just Melissa now." She offers me a hand decorated with more rings than I'm used to seeing on a mannequin, and I admire the tiny sun, moon, and stars artwork on her delicately painted nails. "And you're Veronica, aren't you? A pleasure to see you again!" Her eyes twinkle. "Especially now I don't have to pull rank anymore."

"You were never very good at that, Ms. Barnes."

TJ's drawl is tinged with humor and he leans back as Melissa swats at him, then he surveys her stall with interest.

"You should do some good business today," he says with a grin. "Lots of people here. Plenty who are going to want this sort of stuff."

"Mock all you like, *Timothy*." Melissa arches an eyebrow and I'm amused to see her teasing land. If TJ is going to use her school name, she'll do the same to him. I stifle a laugh. I'm so used to thinking of TJ as, well, *TJ* that even I forget that's not his real name. "I will be glad of any sale I make." She lets out a low sigh. "There's not a lot I miss about Westhaven High, but I certainly wouldn't say no to a nice, steady paycheck right about now." She spies another potential customer circling and ditches us to try and make a sale. I don't blame her, and turn to TJ with a frown.

"When did Ms. Barnes - I mean, Melissa - quit teaching?"

"Oh, ages ago." He lifts his cup to his lips and savors the last of his cider. "A couple of years at least."

"Why? She's surely not old enough to retire, and she was a good teacher." I think back to her hippy-dippy classroom and wince. "Ok, so maybe she wasn't a *great* teacher." I drop my voice to a whisper, not wanting to insult a woman I had generally held in great affection during my teenage years. "But she was nice. I never really appreciated how young she was. She had a whole career in front of her."

TJ rolls his eyes and I sense a story.

"What?"

"You haven't been around, Veronica. I know you think nothing ever changes in sleepy ol' Westhaven but let me tell you, some things have."

"Yes, I can see that." I glance over my shoulder and make out Matt and Anna, still standing close together, their hands entwined in a comfortable, familiar way and I feel my stomach turn over. *How did they end up together? They have absolutely nothing in common! Anna Chambers is the devil in a dress and Matt...Matt...*

"Veronica? You aren't even listening to me, are you?"

TJ's voice is light and teasing but I think I catch a glimmer of hurt in his eyes as I hastily turn back to him with an apologetic smile.

"Tell me again," I insist. "I'm sorry, I got distracted."

"It doesn't matter." He nods towards Melissa's latest customer, murmuring under his breath. "Speaking of things that haven't changed. Once a jerk, always a -"

"Erik!" Melissa greets Erik Villodan with the exact same amount of enthusiasm she showed to me, and I wonder if she treats all her former students that way. My affection for her wanes just a little, as I feel like perhaps she didn't single me out the way I'd thought she did. "How did those anti-inflammatory capsules work out for you? You're taking them just as I specified, right? I know they're only herbal remedies, but -"

"What's this, Ms. Barnes?" TJ leans past me, turning his teasing to our former teacher, but his voice has a slight edge to it. "I wouldn't have to have another word with you about pushing herbal remedies onto people when there are perfectly good proven medicines that an actual pharmacist could suggest?"

"Of course not." Melissa tosses her head, her silvery hair glinting in the late morning sunlight. "I just whipped up a little batch of supplements for Erik, here. Recovery after an injury, wasn't it, dear?"

"Just over-exerted myself a little at the gym." Erik pumps his muscles a couple of times in quick succession, making sure to look my way as he does so. *Gag.* "Good as new now, thanks, Melissa." He winks at her, and for some reason she glows. I guess Erik Villodan's charm isn't lost on every woman in Westhaven. *It's worked on at least two,* I remind myself, wondering again what happened to Christine, and when another unlikely pairing became the new golden couple in town. As Erik drifts away I'm about to ask the question, but TJ has drawn Melissa into an intense discussion of the medicinal properties of herbs and plants, and the importance of drug regulation - a conversation teen-TJ would have roared to hear about - and I find myself on the outside.

"It's nothing dangerous, TJ! Just a little ginger and turmeric, some black pepper, and cinnamon. All things you can buy at a grocery store!"

"But Erik didn't buy them at the grocery store, he bought them from you, and -"

I lay a light hand on TJ's arm, but he doesn't seem to feel it, and I can sense this is a conversation that's likely to run and run. I'm in no mood to get drawn into the middle of it, but I'm also not interested enough to stand by and watch, so I decide to drift away myself, taking in the rest of the sights and sounds of the pie festival and trusting TJ will come and find me when he's exhausted his store of talking points. I'm not worried about Melissa Barnes. If there's one thing I remember about my former teacher it's that she's more than capable of holding her own.

Once I'm out of earshot of TJ and Melissa's spirited discussion, I survey the other tables set up displaying knitted scarves and handmade jewelry worked by eager crafters keen to sell their wares. I make admiring noises to a display of watercolors from a local artist. The views are picture-postcard-perfect and not a bit like *actual* Westhaven, but as I'm about as artistic as a slug, I'm generous with my compliments, and win a beaming smile in return from the painter himself, who is half-obscured by his easel as he continues to work on a picture. He's so enthusiastic in his conversation that I'm half worried I'm about to be painted into his next piece, so I say my farewells and make a hasty retreat.

My gaze strays back to Anna and Matt and I hardly realize I'm staring until an unfamiliar voice reaches my ears.

"They make quite a couple, don't they? I reckon between them they know everybody in town."

I turn, startled to find someone speaking to me that I don't recognize. Like, at all. Then I spot the sheriff's badge glinting in the sunlight and I stiffen, almost without meaning to. He notices, and grins, before sliding his sunglasses off his face to reveal impossibly blue eyes that pin me into place.

"I'm Seth. Or I suppose that should be *Sheriff Seth Foster*." He winks. "But you can call me just Seth. Everybody else does around here."

"Hi," I squeak, finding my voice at last. "I'm Veronica."

"Veronica." He says the name slowly, as if trying it on for size. One swift nod suggests he likes it. "And are you new here in Westhaven, Veronica? Forgive my asking, but I don't think I've seen you around here before, and as a newbie to town myself, it sure would be nice to meet another..."

It's then that I notice the southern twang to his slow drawl.

"Not new." I offer him an apologetic smile. "But it's my first time back in a long time. I grew up here." I draw in a breath, then offer my hand. "Veronica Swan. I'm Ed's daughter. If you know Edgar Swan...?" I can hear the nervous desperation in my voice and try to stifle it, unsure why meeting someone new should get me so rattled when a dozen daily reconnections with people I'd rather forget hasn't.

"Oh, I know Ed." Sheriff Foster grins and I almost do a double take. For a newcomer to Westhaven - for a *sheriff* - he's not bad looking. *Try movie-star handsome*, my conscience prompts. *Drop dead gorgeous. Totally hot.* I straighten, realizing he's said something else that demands an answer.

"Sorry?"

"I just said I didn't realize Ed had a daughter. You don't come back to visit much, do you?"

"I'm sorry?" This time the two words are laden with irritation rather than embarrassment. I remember Pamela Kaufman's none-too-subtle hints about how much my dad was left to cope alone and my skin prickles with annoyance. *I was busy living my life like Dad told me to! It's not like I never saw him. And we talked all the time. I certainly don't need to get a lecture from some guy I've never even met about how to be a better daughter.* I draw in a breath and meet Mr. Blue-Eyes head-on with a stiff smile. "Well, I'm here now. And it looks like I'll be sticking around for a while." I shove thoughts of the pending meeting I've got to have with my boss aside. She's called me twice today and each time I've let the call go to voicemail.

"Veronica! Ronnie!"

I turn my head just in time to see TJ jogging towards me and then can't resist shooting Sheriff Foster an I-told-you-so look. *New in town? I don't think so, buddy.*

"Sorry." TJ grins, a little breathless from his dash to find me. "I got a little side-tracked talking to Melissa. She knows I don't approve of her little off-label herbal medications side gig." He catches sight of the sheriff and straightens. "Nothing illegal in it, of course, but she's kind of encroaching on my turf, you know? How's a guy going to make a living selling Tylenol when she's offering essence of muskrat tea that she claims does just as good a job."

"Essence of muskrat?" Sheriff Foster wrinkles his nose.

"My point exactly." TJ jerks his head towards the tent. "They're going to start judging the pies if you want to head back that way."

"Have you entered the contest?" Sheriff Foster looks a little impressed, and I feel like this will help to bring home exactly how wrong he was to accuse me of being an absent Westhavener, and by extension, an absent daughter.

"I sure have. Isn't that what small-town people do? Take part in small-town activities?" I link arms with TJ, who seems entirely bemused by the frisson of irritation between me and the sheriff, and we walk together toward the center tent.

"Do I want to know what that was about?" he asks in a low voice, once we're out of earshot of the sheriff. I shake my head, trying not to let myself dwell too long on Seth Foster's opinion of me. *I didn't even know Ed had a daughter!* That stings, even though I'm pretty sure he didn't mean it to. *We have to take care of these poor lonely bachelors who don't have anyone else to look after them, don't we?* Pamela Kaufman's obnoxious brightness settles heavily on my shoulders so that it takes an effort to smile at TJ and reassure him that I'm fine, just a little nervous about my pie placing in the contest. There's a crowd of people circling the judges' tent and I see Bella and Erik Villodan's heads bent close together as they have an intense conversation, then I spot Matt, sans Anna, who is busily interrogating George Hamilton and Pamela Kaufman, who I presume is also on the judging panel.

"Typical," I mutter, pointing out Anna's last-minute victory campaign to TJ. "She's just determined to win at everything, isn't she?"

TJ frowns, opening his mouth like he's about to question whether this is really about pie when a piercing scream cuts him short.

"Mr. Hamilton?" Anna shrieks, and the crowd parts as people turn to see what's going on. "Mr. Hamilton? Help! Oh, somebody help! I think he's having trouble breathing!"

I press forward, but others have the same idea and I see bodies shoving this way and that, separating me from TJ and adding to the chaos.

"Give me some room!"

That's Matt's voice, and soon I hear Sheriff Foster from somewhere behind me urging people to stay calm and remain where they are. He pushes his way through the crowd with authority, but even before he can reach the spot where George Hamilton has collapsed I can sense a change in the air. I hear Matt's voice, low and stunned as if he's the only person here.

"I think - I think he might be dead!"

Chapter Five

"What a terrible end to such a wonderful day!"

Somehow I've ended up at Pamela Kaufman's right-hand side, and I robotically pat her on the shoulder, offering her some inefficient comfort.

"I can't believe George is dead! And we were all having such a lovely time!" Pamela sniffs noisily into her handkerchief. "We hadn't even announced the winner of the pie competition yet!"

TJ has been pressed into service and is helping the over-stretched first aid tent to care for the crowd of Westhaven regulars, most of whom are struggling with shock and upset at the horrible events that happened right in front of them. There are a couple of sprained ankles and one person with an unrelated injury, but I watch TJ work and feel a flicker of pride that my old high-school friend has now found his calling. He works through the crowd, his gaze darting around occasionally as if he's looking for someone and I realize, with a flicker of warmth, that he's looking for me. I raise my hand and he spots it. As soon as his last patient is settled he makes a beeline for me, taking control of the Pamela Kaufman situation.

"How are you doing, Mrs. Kaufman?"

"Oh, Timothy." Pamela blows her nose, then sniffs and looks up at him through eyes that swim with tears. "Poor George! Poor everyone! To think of such a thing happening today of all days! And here! It's too terrible!"

"It sure is, Mrs. Kaufman." TJ smiles sympathetically and runs through a quick triage of the older woman. Once he's satisfied himself that Pamela Kaufman is functionally fine, he turns to me.

"Oh, you don't need to check me over," I say, stepping out of his reach before he can ask me to confirm who the president is or check my reflexes. "I'm just fine. Barely even saw anything." I remember the sound of Anna's scream and Matt's breathless *I think he might be dead* and shiver, even though it's still warm out. TJ notices and frowns. "I'm fine!" I insist, before feeling my phone start to vibrate insistently in the back pocket of my jeans. I reach for it, momentarily dumbfounded when I see it isn't a call or a string of messages but an alarm. An alarm I now remember setting earlier this morning. "But I do have to get out of here!" I turn the phone to TJ, who can't see the significance. I smile and remind him of the good news I greeted him with when we first met today. "I'm going to get my dad from the hospital, remember? They said he's made such good progress they can discharge him today. Right now, in fact."

"That's great." TJ smiles, but the expression doesn't quite meet his eyes.

"You don't think it'll be a problem, do you?" I scan the crowd for Sheriff Foster. "It's not like I have anything else to add. I didn't see any more than anyone else."

TJ is quiet and when I look at him a shadow has settled over his features that is slow to shift.

"What about you? You must have been closer than I was after we got separated by the crowd." I wonder if this explains my friend's strange mood. It must be horrible to see someone die, especially when it's someone you know. And TJ might work in a hospital but it's not like he's on the ward all the time.

He's not a doctor. I grab his hand and squeeze, which makes him look at me. "Are you ok?"

"I'm fine." He squeezes back, looking more like himself already. "Come on, let's get out of here. You're right. Neither of us can do anything else to help out now."

We turn and walk towards the park gates but only make it a few paces before a shout makes us stop.

"Hey! Where do you think you're going?"

I turn and feel a spark of irritation as one of Sheriff Foster's deputies comes bustling toward us. Sheena Dell was self-important as a school-kid. Somehow as an adult she's even worse.

"This is a crime scene, you know," she says, her gaze settling suspiciously on TJ. "You can't just walk off. We need to take everyone's statements."

"Everyone?" I raise my eyebrows. "There's a crowd of people here, Sheena. You're going to get a hundred versions of exactly the same thing. George Hamilton had a medical episode and died."

"A medical episode?" Sheena matches my scorn with some of her own. "And what kind of medical episode is that?"

"Why don't you ask one of the people who was standing right next to him at the time?" I shoot back. "Instead of quizzing us about it? We were in the middle of the crowd. What are we going to be able to add to the overall picture other than that it was chaotic?"

"But -"

"Is everything ok here, Deputy?"

At last. Sanity - in the shape of Sheriff Foster - comes to join us. His sunglasses are firmly in place against the bright sun and even though I can't see his piercing blue eyes I can feel them fix on me.

"Ms. Swan. Something the matter?"

"I have to leave." I turn away from Sheena and face Seth square on. "I have someplace I need to be right now."

"Don't we all." The sheriff smiles sardonically. "Unfortunately, Deputy Dell here is right. There's been a serious incident here and until we get to the bottom of it we're asking everyone to stay where they are. You don't object to doing your civic duty, now, do you?" His gaze strays past me to TJ, who looks a lot more nervous than he did a minute ago. "How about you?"

"Neither of us saw anything," I declare, answering on TJ's behalf as well as mine. "We were in the middle of the crowd. I suggested to Sheena -"

"Deputy *Dell*," she squawks.

"I suggested to Deputy Dell that you would have more success speaking to the people closest to Mr. Hamilton at the time. Physically standing right next to him, I mean."

"Such as?" Sheriff Foster is looking at me carefully and I admit, if I had anything to hide, his scrutiny might make me a little nervous. *It's a good job I'm an open book, at least where this is concerned.*

"Well, Anna Chambers was with him when he keeled over." Sheena sniffs and I try to ignore her. "And Matthew Taylor." I wonder if anyone else can hear the strange wobble in my voice as I mention Matt's name. "There were others, but if I were you, I'd start there."

"If you were me." There's something vaguely mocking in Sheriff Foster's words and I try not to let it unnerve me.

"I also wouldn't insist on everyone standing around here waiting to give statements. Get the information you need and send people home." I grow in confidence as I speak. "We're all busy people, Sheriff. I can't be the only one with somewhere else I have to be right now."

"And where is that?"

"The hospital." It's TJ who offers this answer, and I turn, almost surprised to see he's still standing next to me, he's been so quiet. "We're going to pick up Ronnie's dad. He's getting discharged today."

"Right now." I pull my phone out of my pocket and sure enough there's a message from my father sitting right there on the display. I tilt it towards the sheriff, allowing him to read the short note.

I'm ready to go. Can you pick me up?

There's a moment of silence and I can almost hear the cogs whirring in Sheriff Foster's head. I fully expect him to pull rank and demand we stay put, but in an instant his demeanor shifts. He straightens, he smiles, and he actually waves us off.

"Well, I certainly wouldn't want to be responsible for Edgar Swan staying in hospital longer than he needs to. You're free to go." I hesitate, then feel TJ grab my hand and start to move. We've made it all of three paces when the sheriff's next words reach us. "Only don't go too far, Veronica. Or you, TJ. We might need to talk to you again."

There's something ominous in his voice that seems to land more with TJ than it does with me. My friend's grip on my hand tightens and when I glance at his face it's pale. Something has him spooked.

• • • •

"HOME SWEET HOME!"

When Dad flops down into his favorite armchair I'm not sure which of us is happier to be home at last.

"Did you move something?" He's peering suspiciously around the room. "What's different?"

"I tidied." I pull a footstool over to where Dad's sitting and ease his feet up onto it, swapping his shoes for a pair of brand-new slippers I picked up in honor of his homecoming. "And I cleaned. Honestly, Dad. Why didn't you tell me you were struggling to keep the place up?"

"I wasn't struggling." Dad bristles. "This place was just fine." He stretches forward and ruffles my hair. "But thanks all the same." He inhales. "What's that smell? Have you been baking?"

My stomach lurches and when I straighten it's all I can do to force my features into some vague approximation of a smile. I haven't told Dad what happened at the festival, but I'm going to have to do it soon before he finds out from someone else. *Try to avoid any sudden shocks*, Dr. Stephens said. *How am I supposed to tell him about George Hamilton's sudden and unexpected death without it being a shock?*

"Oh, hey, wasn't it the pie festival today? You haven't told me how you did." Dad chuckles. "Who am I kidding? *My* daughter? You'll have got first place with whatever you made, I'm sure of it." He's teasing me: Dad knows I've never been any good at baking, but he seems to read something in my response before I've even managed to figure out what to say. "What happened?"

"Dad, it's about Mr. Hamilton. He -"

"George was one of the judges, wasn't he?" Dad frowns. "Well, if he marked you down just over our little falling out over cards, he'll have me to deal with. Where's my phone? Bring it here and I'll tell that old fool what I think of him -"

"Dad." I take his hand in both of mine and something about the gesture makes him realise something is wrong. "Mr. Hamilton was ill at the festival. He - well, I don't know what happened. But it was very sudden. There was nothing any of us could do. He died."

My dad doesn't say anything at first. His lips twitch as he tries to find words and he blinks a few times quickly before speaking, his voice little more than a whisper.

"George is dead?"

I nod and feel Dad's hand slip away from me.

"Well, that'll certainly put a dampener on Thursday night poker." He rubs his nose. "I suppose I don't have to pay what I owe him though, so that's something."

"Dad!"

He smiles at me then, a sad smile that lets me know he's joking to hide the fact he's saddened by the sudden and unexpected death of a friend.

"Was it a heart attack?"

His voice is low and I can see that he's not sure he wants to know the answer. Again, Dr. Stephens' warnings ring in my head about just how lucky Dad is to still be here.

"No." I frown. "I don't think so." I rake back through my memories and try to remember what I saw happen, but before I can conjure up a clear picture there's a knock at the front door. "That'll be the welcoming committee." I drop a kiss on my dad's thin cheek and smile, hoping that whoever is at the door is someone who can offer us a distraction and lift the mood a little. As soon as I see who's standing on the step, though, I hesitate.

"Yoo-hoo!" Pamela Kaufman has seen me. There's no hiding now, and I arrange my features into a smile I hope is warmer and more welcoming than I feel right now.

"Mrs. Kaufman! What can I do for you?" She certainly looks a lot happier than when I last saw her. I suppose the shock of the morning has worn off a little by now, and she's shifted right back into Women's League mode. Serving others - whether they want it or not - isn't the worst coping method in the world.

"Well, I heard that dear Edgar has just come from the hospital and I thought to myself, Pamela, the last thing those poor people are going to want to do is cook. So I came prepared!" She thrusts a new, full casserole dish at me, then winks as I take it from her. "Tuna casserole today! I trust you enjoyed the pot roast?"

I smile and make a mental note to keep Pamela out of the kitchen and away from the fridge, so she won't see that her pot roast is still sitting there entirely untouched.

"Who is it, Ronnie?" Dad calls from the living room, and before I have time to answer him, Pamela steps into the house and announces herself.

"It's just me, dear! Pamela Kaufman! I wanted to come and see for myself how you're doing." She pats me on the shoulder and sails on into the house, leaving me standing in the doorway clutching a very heavy casserole dish. I reluctantly heave it into a better position and close the front door, before making my way into the kitchen. I can hear Pamela chattering away and my dad's responses are quite bright and interested which suggests he's pleased to see her. Rolling my eyes, I hastily dump out the old, uneaten pot roast and put the tuna casserole in its place before hiding the empty dish in our dishwasher and filling a kettle.

"I'll get us some drinks, shall I?"

"Oh, that would be lovely, dear, thank you!" Pamela calls back, with all the authority that would suggest she's quite at home here. Not for the first time, I wonder if there's something going on between her and my father, and when I hear his low chuckle accompanied by her high-pitched giggle I cringe and hastily fill two glasses with iced tea. I don't have time to wait for the kettle to boil.

"Here we are!" I hurry back into the living room and pass a glass each to Dad and Pamela, before sinking into the sofa. Pamela is sitting in the armchair opposite Dad, and I begin to feel like I've interrupted something when Pamela turns to me.

"I wanted to check on you after the festival this morning, too. I know I was shocked by what happened and then I somehow lost track of you, Veronica, dear. Wasn't it dreadful?"

"Ronnie just told me," Dad broke in. "George had some kind of episode?"

Pamela nods, taking a slow, sad sip of her tea.

"Well, he was supposed to be judging the pies, you see. I guess it's always a risk."

"He choked on something?" I ask, glad to finally get a straight answer. Pamela leans forward and puts her glass down on the table in between us. She looks at me with a frown.

"No, dear. Didn't you hear? It was such a tragic accident. He had an allergic reaction. To cinnamon."

"From one of the pies?"

"They aren't saying as much, of course." Pamela shakes her head. "But he was usually so careful! And all the entrants had their ingredients listed, so he knew what to avoid. But I suppose there's always a risk..."

My heart sinks and I feel as if the walls of our spacious living room are closing in around me. George Hamilton died from an allergic reaction to cinnamon. I remember him complaining about that very allergy when we were in the diner. My misery over this tragic end is compounded by another - worse - thought that makes my hands shake and I fold them both in my lap, praying neither Pamela nor my dad notice. They're distracted, talking about other things, but my mind is stuck on this one fact.

The pumpkin pie I baked used plenty of cinnamon. Is it possible - just maybe - that I'm the one who killed George Hamilton?

Chapter Six

I didn't expect to sleep much the first night Dad was home from the hospital, but as it turns out worrying about him is only part of the reason I'm up before the sun is. I creep quietly around my room, trying to get ready without disturbing him.

"Is that you, Ronnie?"

Dad's sleepy voice floats up to greet me as soon as I hit the first creaking step on my way downstairs.

"Yes," I whisper, then realize if he's up there's no need to keep being so quiet. "Why are you awake?" I hurry down the rest of the stairs and into the living room, going straight to the temporary bed we made up on the sofa for him to use as he recovers. "Are you ok? Are you in any pain?"

"Yes." Dad smiles. "And no." He yawns. "I've spent the last few days sleeping or resting and honestly, I think I've got my fill." He wriggles around and I help him to sit up, perching next to him on the edge of the sofa. "Where are you off to?" He notices my outfit choice for the day and stifles a laugh. "Don't tell me my only daughter has become a gym bunny! Any other big city habits you've developed while you've been away?"

"I'm going for a run," I say, acting like that's a sentence I've ever uttered before in my life. I straighten the waistband of my tracksuit, then pull my ponytail tighter. "And there's a couple of bits we need to pick up from the pharmacy. I was hoping to get out and back before you woke up." I smooth his hair out of his eyes. "Did I disturb you? I'm sorry."

"You didn't," Dad insists. "I've been lying here for ages waiting to be allowed to get up." His eyes twinkle. "What do you think? Do you trust your ol' dad to be left to his own devices for a little bit this morning?"

"That depends." I match his mischievous smile with one of my own. "Can I trust you to do what the doctor said?" I list off the instructions. "No walking upstairs, no lifting anything heavy, no physical labor of any kind..."

He rolls his eyes but grumblingly complies and I hug him.

"Good! I won't be long."

"I'll be here," Dad grumbles something else but I choose to ignore it. It was always going to be difficult to shepherd my usually independent and active father through his recovery but now I've got the added complication of George Hamilton on my conscience. "Enjoy your run!"

I assure him I will, but I only actually jog a few paces before sliding back into little more than a speed walk. And I turn in the opposite direction from any of the popular trails around Westhaven. I'm headed to one place and one place only. *I'm going to take the same advice I gave Sheriff Foster. If I want to find out what happened to George, then I'm going to speak to the people who were standing right next to him when he collapsed.*

I arrive at the Slice of Life diner almost before I expect to and am pleased to see the lights are already on, even though the sign is still turned to *closed* and when I try the door, it's locked. I hesitate before knocking, wondering if I ought to come back later, but then I remember I don't want to leave Dad alone for too long, and I still have work of my own to catch up on that keeps getting neglected. I need to finally return one of my boss's numerous calls, and it's not like I don't have other things to do today. I'm still waffling in indecision when I hear the keys turn in the lock and the door swings open, framing a very sleepy-looking Matt, who is still midway through eating a slice of toast. His apron is hanging from his neck loose and untied, and he fumbles for the strings with his free hand.

"We aren't open yet," he mutters as he swallows his last bite of breakfast. "But seeing as it's you..." He smiles gruffly and jerks his head, inviting me in before he closes and locks the door again behind me. I realize we haven't spoken since yesterday and somehow, knowing exactly who he's currently in a relationship is making me rethink everything I thought I knew about my oldest friend. He seems to act differently around me, too. There's no hug, no teasing, no laughter. He does smile, at least, as he makes his way further into the diner.

"So what can I get for you? Coffee?"

"Ooh, that would be perfect, babe! Can you make it three?"

I freeze as Anna Chambers swings nonchalantly into the diner from the back door marked *private*, the door that leads to a flight of stairs that go directly to the apartment overhead that I guess Matt still lives in. *And not alone.*

"Veronica!" Anna spots me a moment after I spot her and her smile dims, but only for a moment. Soon it's plastered neatly back in place, and she follows Matt around to the coffee machine, counting out three paper cups before eyeing me and adding a fourth to the line she's making. She talks to Matt as if I'm not even there, but she isn't making any effort to conceal her words, so I guess it's nothing very private. "I'm going to take these coffees over to the Villodans. After everything that happened yesterday I just think they need a little extra care from their friends, don't you?" She glances at me. "They were George Hamilton's neighbors, you know."

I nod, but Matt offers a response very like the one I would have if I'd been able to find my voice.

"They might be his next-door neighbors but they weren't exactly close."

"That's hardly the point!" Anna pouts, her voice taking on a whiny, high-pitched note. "Are you going to make these coffees or not? Because I just wanted to do a nice thing, and -"

"Of course." I can't see Matt, but if I didn't know better I'd think he was speaking through clenched teeth. He undermines it by turning and kissing Anna full on the mouth, though, and I remain grateful I haven't eaten anything yet today. Even with nearly twenty-four hours to process the idea that Matt and Anna are a couple I still can't quite believe it.

"Thank you." Anna turns to me, her voice cold. "And I'm assuming Veronica wants one as well. That's why you're here, right?"

I nod and open my mouth to say more, but Anna cuts me off before I get the chance.

"I'm going to spend some time with Bella and Erik, just to make sure they're ok. It's so awful to lose someone so close to you so suddenly."

"I don't suppose Erik will mind all that much," Matt mutters. "He won't have anyone to argue with anymore about that boundary fence, will he?"

"As if either of them will be thinking about that right now!" Anna is irritated, but when she catches sight of me, she shuffles closer to Matt and softens her tone to something honeyed and sweet. "I just think we need to be there for them while they process all this. And they want to check up on us, too. I mean, we were right there when...when it happened." She drops her voice to a whisper that's all but drowned out when Matt uses the milk frother. "Don't forget Sheriff Foster wants to speak to us today. I said we'd go in after lunch. You can get someone to cover here, can't you?"

"Uh..."

"I can do it!" I offer, stepping forward. Matt is so startled he catches his hand on the steamer and curses at the burn. He turns to look at me. "Are you sure?"

"Do you mind if I bring Dad?" I offer a wary smile. "He's already going stir-crazy at home. I reckon if I can prop him up in one of the booths here it'll help us both. I can keep an eye on him while I take care of things here, and he can have a steady stream of other people to talk to." I pause. "And anyway, it won't be for long, will it?"

Matt hesitates, but I can see he's tempted. He glances at Anna, who hastily arranges her features into a smile.

"There! It's all sorted. You and I can go and speak to the sheriff and Veronica can look after this place." Her gaze travels to me. "You can manage to wait tables for an hour, can't you? Not too much of a come-down from your high-flying city career?"

Ouch. I smile, determined to show Anna that her barbs don't hurt me anymore.

"I can manage just fine. It'll be nice to spend some time here again and I don't suppose much has really changed. The Slice is always the same as ever, like most of Westhaven."

"I don't know," Anna says, as she carefully puts lids onto the four coffees Matt has made. She hands one to me, then stacks the others carefully to carry out to her car. "One or two things have changed around here. For the better, right, babe?"

She angles her face towards Matt and he kisses her quickly on the cheek before turning back to the coffee machine, and I wonder if he's as happy with these changes as Anna is.

• • • •

"ALRIGHT. WHAT ARE YOU really doing here?"

Once Matt and I are alone, he brings his mug of black coffee around to my side of the counter and pulls out a stool for me, before sliding onto one of his own.

"I know the coffee here is good, but it isn't that good." He takes a noisy sip of his drink, then seems to notice, for the first time, what I'm wearing. "Since when do you own lycra?"

"Since I discovered it's super comfy to wear when working from home." I tug at the collar, undoing the zip an inch or two so I can breathe. "And because I needed an excuse to leave the house for a few minutes. *Going for a run* passed my dad's sniff test a lot better than *going to do some sleuthing.*"

"Sleuthing?" Matt's eyebrows raise. "About what, exactly?"

"Yesterday." I pick at the paper sleeve on my cup, unsure quite how to phrase my next question. "You were right there when Mr. Hamilton...when he..."

"When he died?" Matt reaches out a hand to mine, stilling the nervous action. "Yes. I was standing next to him, with Anna." He grimaces. "Hence why we have to go see Sheriff Foster today to give him our statements. Again." He lets go of my hand and takes a sip of his drink. "I guess he wants to see if we've changed our stories."

"And what is your story?" I look at him. "What happened?"

"Well, you were there too, weren't you? You saw it."

I shake my head.

"There was such a crowd I barely saw anything. I just heard Anna scream, and then I saw you and her try to hold onto Mr. Hamilton as he collapsed to the ground. And then I heard that he'd died." I draw in a shaky breath. "What happened?"

Matt shrugs his shoulders, his expression clouding as he revisits a memory he wishes he didn't possess.

"You want all the gory details?"

"I just...I want to know what killed him." I bite my lip. *I want to know it wasn't something I did.*

"It wasn't a heart attack," Matt says quickly, seeing my eagerness to know the truth and misreading the cause of it. "If that's what you're worried about. His heart was just fine. No, this was..." He shudders. "It was like he couldn't breathe. The first aider said they'd seen it once or twice, but never as bad as this. Anapha-ana-" He struggles over the word.

"Anaphylaxis? Like an allergic reaction?"

"Right." Matt nods. "I guess the cinnamon finally got to him." He scratches his nose. "I don't know how, though. He was always so careful. I mean, remember the other day? I baked a whole new batch of pancakes so he would be safe to eat them. He was always good at asking if something had cinnamon in it. He didn't trust other people to remember for him. And he had one of those - what do you call them? Epi-pens. Only he didn't have it with him yesterday." Matt shakes his head. "Nor did the first aider. She was really cut up about that because usually they keep one in case of bee stings and things. I guess someone will get an earful for not checking the kit was fully stocked with everything they might need for a big community event like the pie festival." He lifts his head. "Congratulations, by the way. You were the winner."

"What?"

"Your pumpkin pie." He grins. "Or should I say *our* pumpkin pie? It took first place. First time in years that Anna's cherry pie hasn't walked it and let me tell you she was not happy...although, with everything that happened of course nobody cares about who won the pie contest."

I drop my gaze, embarrassed at the tiny prickle of pride I feel at besting Anna in one area, at least. I immediately repent, especially as this only compounds my earlier fear.

"Matt." I can hear the anxiety in my voice, and from the way Matt turns suddenly to look at me I can tell he does too. "I used cinnamon in my pumpkin pie. Well, it was in the spice mix." I'm not sure how to force my next words out but somehow I manage it. "You don't think - you can't think - that Mr. Hamilton tried a slice, can you? That it was our pie that - that killed him?"

Matt's features are blank, but I can tell he's thinking carefully about this, turning the idea over and over in his mind before answering.

"No." He shakes his head, then repeats himself, firmly. "No. He would have known that pumpkin spice is almost all cinnamon. And it was labeled." He smiles. "Trust me. Your prize-winning pumpkin pie is not responsible for George Hamilton's demise."

I should be encouraged by this. I am. But if it wasn't my pie that caused Mr. Hamilton's allergic reaction, what did?

Matt has an answer for that too, it seems. I feel his gaze on me, and I'm almost surprised at how cold his tone of voice has become when he speaks again.

"You're still pretty close with TJ, right? He's the guy who supplies most of the drugs in this town."

"Matt, he's a pharmacist." I feel like we're all back in high school and Matt is lecturing me over my choice of friends. "That's literally his job."

"Well, maybe he *literally* made a mistake." He nods towards the booth where I had last enjoyed a cup of coffee with George Hamilton. "Remember when you guys ate those pancakes? George joked that he had so many pills for things he rattled. Maybe one of those is what caused his allergy flare. And if anyone is going to know about that, it's TJ. He was right on the scene at the festival too, wasn't he? Conveniently."

"If we're going to talk convenience then I'm going to remind you that it was you and your girlfriend who were closest to Mr. Hamilton when he died."

"And what would either of us have to gain from his death?"

I shrug my shoulders.

"What would TJ?"

"I don't know." Matt takes a pointed sip of his coffee and I feel the last bit of our earlier rapport vanish. "You'd have to ask him about that."

Chapter Seven

Visiting the pharmacy was next on my list of jobs to do, anyway. I need to fill Dad's latest script from the hospital. *That's my reason for visiting*, I tell myself. *But if I happen to see TJ there and we just happen to end up discussing what went on yesterday...*

I push open the door and walk into the small pharmacy on Westhaven's main street and am startled to see how many people are standing around in here. Who knew there was a busy time for picking up medication? I patiently join the back of the queue and wait as one unfamiliar - and entirely overwhelmed - female pharmacist hurries to fill orders for a crowd of increasingly impatient patients. I check my watch. Dad will be fine with me waiting a bit, I'm sure. I work my phone free of the pocket of my leggings all the same and tap out a text message.

Held up at the pharmacist. How are you feeling?

I see three dots flash up almost immediately and am unsurprised by Dad's quick response.

Like I'm going to die of boredom if I have to spend the next few days laid up like this. He evidently regrets the grumpy tone that comes through even via text and follows up with a winky-face emoji. I tap out a reply.

Well, if you stay put and keep resting this morning maybe you can help me hold down the fort at the Slice later on today. And by "help me" I mean "sit in one spot and quietly watch the world go by". Thoughts?

That prompts a string of emojis in response. Thumbs up, smiley faces, enthusiasm all around. I smile and shove my phone away again, pleased that my offer of help to Matt this morning will also help my dad feel less like an invalid and more like his old self. He still doesn't know that I know that he's sold the business outright to Matt, and I wonder how long it'll take him to tell me. I sigh, thinking about how quickly all my questions for my dad have been shoved aside by what happened yesterday. *Well, I can wait for answers from Dad. I'm keener to get a few answers about what happened to Mr. Hamilton before -*

"Next!"

The queue in front of me has been gradually dispersing while I've been lost in my thoughts, and the bark of the woman at the counter makes me jump. I look around, surprised to find I'm alone in the small pharmacy.

"How can I help you?" She softens her tone a little seeing my expression and even manages a smile. I hand over the script I need to fill and peer past her to see if there's any sign of my friend.

"Where's TJ?"

"Your guess is as good as mine. He was supposed to be working here this morning, but instead, I got called in to cover. It's a nightmare. I can't find anything in this place!" She turns from stressed to downright frosty, and near enough snatches the script from my outstretched hand, scanning it quickly. "I'll fill this for you but it'll take me a minute to get everything together. Are you ok to hang on for a few minutes?" She's already pacing around the back of the store, searching the shelves for the items I need, so I nod and settle in to wait. I'm worried, but not that worried. The TJ I remember used to view school attendance as an option, rather than a necessity. It's strangely comforting to see not everything about my old friend has changed during our time apart. I pull out my phone again, this time tapping out a message to TJ to warn him that his colleague is two difficult customer interactions away from making a voodoo doll of him and suggesting he might like to get his butt into work before too much more time passes. I watch the message move to sent, but there's no immediate reply. It isn't even showing as *received* yet, and I feel my confidence in my friend's wellbeing dip just a bit. I check the time, but I can't delay getting back to Dad any longer. I tap out another message and hope TJ will reply soon, if only to put my overactive imagination at ease. I'm just about done typing as the door to the pharmacy swings open and two women I vaguely recognize step inside. I smile and greet them with a warm Westhaven welcome, but I'm not too disappointed when they choose to talk to each other instead of me. There's only so much polite small talk I can handle this early in the morning. My stomach rumbles and I remember I haven't even had breakfast yet.

"Well, *I* heard they'd been trying to get rid of him for years. Nothing stuck. He was like a fixture in that place."

"A grumpy fixture."

"Oh, he wasn't so bad. Do you remember that afternoon he decided we could all have class outside because it was too nice to stay holed up in a classroom all day?" The woman sighs and I risk a glance her way. Are they talking about who I think they're talking about? Mr. Hamilton was well known for relocating his class outdoors at the slightest opportunity, arguing that fresh air and sunshine were as important for learning as actual studying. It led to a lot of goofing off, of course, but he was strict enough and well-liked enough that the majority of us kids still managed to knuckle down and work when he wanted us to. A wave of sadness sweeps over me when I think that George Hamilton isn't only no longer a teacher, he's no longer anything. He's gone, forever. *And all because of a stupid allergic reaction to something he never should have eaten anyway!*

The two women waiting near me have fallen silent and I abruptly shift my posture, trying to look conspicuously like I'm not listening to them. Sure enough, in another moment, they begin their whispered conversation again.

"As I say, they tried for years to get rid of him. Well, it's worked now, hasn't it? He's out of their hair forever."

"But he already retired, Mae. Why would they then go the extra mile and *kill him*?" She pauses. "And who are *they,* anyway? You can't mean to say Miranda Ayres is a murderess in her spare time?"

Miranda Ayres? Where do I know that name from? And murder? This is getting out of hand. People are starting to speculate - wildly - and if there's one thing Westhaven is famous for it's letting rumors run rampant. There have been plenty of scandals that blew up out of proportion because nobody in this town can keep their mouths shut.

"I bet someone muddled his medication. An old man like that, I expect he was on all sorts of pills. And the school retired him on medical grounds, didn't they? I wonder if someone had access to his medical history, then they'd know exactly what to do."

I check my phone, but there's no reply from either TJ or my dad. I know I was perfectly happy to wait for the pharmacist to take her time filling my script but now I'm starting to get antsy. Rumors are swirling, and more than one of them is attaching itself to my friend - and he's not even here to defend himself!

"Here we are!" The substitute pharmacist emerges at last, clutching a paper bag stuffed with pills and potions that will hopefully speed my father's recovery. Her smile falls when she sees more clients after me, and I gratefully take the parcel and hurry past my neighbors, barely slowing to bid them farewell. I feel sure I hear their whispering start up before I'm even out of earshot and I wonder if mine is the next name they're going to weave into their fiction of what really happened to Mr. Hamilton. *Veronica Swan...just back in town...had coffee with the victim only a couple of days before he died...no way she's not involved!* I pick up my pace, but instead of taking the path towards home I make a detour. I shouldn't add to my errands now, but I decide I can spare five minutes - especially if doing so might help stop some of these rumors before they start to take root.

• • • •

"MS. SWAN."

If Sheriff Foster is surprised to see me turn up at the station he doesn't show it. He does look different in work clothes - sans sunglasses - but somehow the pale overhead lights accentuate his tan rather than washing him out. I tug at my sleeve and wish I'd had the foresight to get changed. Lycra can be very unforgiving, especially at still-early-o'clock in the morning.

"Sheriff. I wondered if there'd been any progress in discovering what happened yesterday."

"Oh, you mean the crime scene you were desperate to get away from only minutes after it happened?"

I'm taken aback, even more so when he offers a laconic smile and I realize he's teasing me.

"How's your dad? Happy to be home, I'll bet."

"I - yes." I nod. "He is. There's still a long way to go, but -"

"Better he does his healing up at home instead of in the hospital. You give him my best, won't you?"

"I will."

Sheriff Foster has turned and is walking away from me before I realize I've been dismissed.

"Wait!" I hurry after him, only to stop when he does, using his own body as a shield to keep me from making any further progress into the sheriff's station.

"Is something the matter, Ms. Swan?"

"You didn't answer my question! Did you figure out what happened to George?"

"He died, Ms. Swan." The Sheriff's eyebrows raise. "I believe you saw it happen."

"Well, yes, but -"

"Then you probably know more about it than I do. Maybe I should be the one asking you the questions. I haven't forgotten you avoided giving us your statement yesterday. You and your friend TJ."

Something in the way he says TJ's name makes me nervous and reminds me of the reason I came here in the first place.

"That's actually what I wanted to talk to you about."

"Your statement?" He turns his head, surveying a line of closed doors. "Very well. I'm sure we can find somewhere private to talk for a moment if you -"

"No, I mean -" I'm getting frazzled and I'm fairly sure Sheriff Foster can sense it. He's probably planned it that way. If he would just let me get a whole sentence out without interrupting me, maybe we could both make some progress. "I want to talk to you about TJ. About what people are saying about him. It's not true!"

Now Sheriff Foster chooses to stay silent, and his expectant expression is almost more infuriating than his jumping in to cut me off. At last, he speaks but his tone is softer, like he's inviting me to answer.

"And what are people saying about him?"

"That he was somehow responsible for what happened to Mr. Hamilton." I shake my head. "He wasn't. TJ had nothing to do with what happened," I say. "He was with me the whole time. Well, not the whole time..."

"Then you can't give him an alibi for the time just before Mr. Hamilton's illness?"

"Not entirely - but that doesn't mean -"

"I assume you were aware that he and Mr. Hamilton were engaged in quite the argument before the pie festival began?"

"What? Of course not." I blink, wondering what to make of this. I lost track of TJ when we were looking at Melissa Barnes's stall, but I hadn't seen him even pass the time of day with George Hamilton. "That can't be right. TJ wouldn't argue with anyone." That isn't strictly true, and I feel my cheeks flush, certain I look guilty as sin to the canny sheriff. To his credit, he says nothing but continues to stare at me like he's seeing right into my very soul. "I don't know anything about an argument," I say slowly, carefully forming each word to be sure he hears and understands them. "I do know TJ wouldn't hurt anyone. He's a good person. He tried to help -"

"And do you know where TJ is now, Ms. Swan?" There's a low, dangerous note in the sheriff's voice, and I'm sure he knows what answer I'm going to give before I give it. I hesitate, trying to find any way around admitting the truth, but there is none. *Not unless I want to lie.* "Ms. Swan?"

"No," I admit, miserably. "I don't know where TJ is now. But that doesn't mean he had anything to do with George Hamilton's death. Why would he? They were friends! George Hamilton was a fixture of Westhaven. TJ would never do anything to hurt him. Nobody would."

"Somebody would, Ms. Swan. Somebody did." Sheriff Foster gives me a steely look. "And I'm going to find out who."

Chapter Eight

"How are you feeling, Dad?"

"About the same as I was when you last asked me five minutes ago." Sitting in a booth directly in view of the coffee machine, Dad's head is bent over the newspaper, as he slowly works his way through the day's puzzle page. He's three clues into the crossword when he looks up. "Actually..."

"Yes?" I drop the cloth I'm holding and hurry out from behind the counter. "What's wrong?"

"I'm a little hungry." He peers past me towards the glass-fronted pastry cabinet. "Reckon you can slice me off a little piece of that carrot cake?"

"Dad!"

"What? It has carrots in it! It's healthy!"

"You can have a piece of toast," I tell him, turning back to the counter and feeling my heart rate slowly regulate itself again after the moment of panic I just went through. "And another coffee. Decaf!" This provokes yet another round of whispered grumbles and I turn back to glare at my father. It's the same look he perfected on me when I was a teenager, so I know just how effective it can be. "Doctor's orders," I say, quietly reminding him of the regime Dr. Stephens has him on as part of his recovery. *No caffeine, no alcohol, no junk food. No fun!*

Dad sighs but nods obediently before returning to frown at his crossword puzzle. I know he's glad to be out of the house and I'm pleased to see how much just being in the diner has lifted his spirits. We might have to spend a bit more time here even when I'm not helping Matt out.

The door opens and another customer bustles in, startling first to see me instead of Matt behind the counter, and then making a beeline for Dad.

This is another reason he's happy being here today, I think, stifling a smile at the evident delight that appears on Dad's face as another friend and neighbor hurries to his side. *He can hold court with an endless stream of admirers.* I plate up his toast and pour his coffee, taking both over to the table and pausing to see if the new arrival would like anything.

"Just a coffee, dear, please!" Jennifer Gould says, without even pausing for breath before she turns back to Dad. "You're looking so well, Edgar. Although I suppose you should do, with your daughter taking such good care of you."

"She is." Dad grimaces, before taking a minuscule bite of his toast. He catches my eye and obediently takes another bite, smiling as he swallows. "And it makes all the difference being able to come and sit and do my recovering here, with plenty of company."

I smile to myself as I go to make Jennifer's coffee. It's going to be a challenge to persuade Dad to come home with me once Matt comes back from his interview with Sheriff Foster. I glance at my watch, trying to calculate how long he and Anna have been gone. Recalling how quickly the sheriff dealt with me this morning, I can't help but wonder just how intense this particular interview is getting. *What would either of us have to gain from Mr. Hamilton's death?* Matt had asked me. *Nothing. Just like TJ, and yet plenty of people in Westhaven seem happy to hang the blame for it on his shoulders.* As I wait for the coffee to brew I check my phone, worried that my friend still hasn't replied to my messages. He's either ignoring me - which is bad - or he's unable to answer, which is worse. The machine next to me beeps and I automatically pour a steaming cup of coffee for Jennifer, adding the cream and sugar I know she likes, before taking it over to where she's sitting, regaling Dad with stories of people she knew whose lives completely turned around after their own health crises.

"...and then there's Sam. He overhauled everything! Took up swimming, he did. In the lake near his house. Francesca, she became a vegan, and instantly started sending me videos of little baby pigs and cows and happy little chickens and informing me that *meat is murder* three times a day." Jennifer purses her lips. "We aren't quite so close these days."

"I don't think you need to worry about Dad becoming a health zealot," I tell the older lady as I hand over her coffee. "It's as much as I can do to keep the majority of his vices at bay."

"Vices?" Jennifer tuts. "What vices? He's an angel, your dad. You ought to be grateful you get to keep him around a little longer! After what happened yesterday..."

And just like that the conversation turns back to George Hamilton, and I'm treated to Jennifer Gould's own personal opinion of what happened.

"Well, my Peter was there, and *he* thinks..."

Surprisingly, Mr. Gould's opinion is similar to his wife's, and their consensus is that somebody mislabelled their pie entry, poisoning George entirely by accident.

"Do you think so?" I try to sound neutral but can't quite hide the nervous *yip* in my voice that makes Dad look at me with concern. "I hope not. How awful."

"Well, you never can be too careful. I know George would avoid anything that was obviously spiced with cinnamon - apple pie, pumpkin pie, those kinds. But it's the kind of ingredient that gets added to everything, often without people realizing it. Like vanilla!" She pulls a face. "Gives me terrible headaches, that does, and it's in all sorts of things you wouldn't think!"

"It's a bit more serious when your reaction makes you drop dead though, isn't it?" Dad asks, quietly.

"That's why I think the medics had something to do with it. They ought to have had those - what do you call them?" She makes a jabbing motion with her hand. "Those pen things to help stop an allergic reaction. We have to keep one in the house whenever our grandchildren come because the youngest one can't be near a peanut without breaking out in hives." She leans closer to Dad, dropping her voice to a whisper. "It's suspicious that there wasn't one to be found in the whole first-aid tent, don't you think?"

"Who was in charge of that? I bet they feel dreadful about the oversight."

"No idea. But mark my words, they'll have some questions to answer..."

The cheerful slice-of-pie clock on the wall chimes the hour and Jennifer leaps to her feet.

"Goodness! Is that the time?" She checks her watch to be sure, then dashes for the door. "I'm late!"

"Your coffee!" I call after her, but she's already gone, leaving her barely-sipped cup on the table. *And she never paid for it, either!* I clean up and get back to work, pleased when a couple of new customers come in, paying upfront, and taking their

orders to the table themselves. Another friend or two stops by
Dad's booth, offering him distraction and conversation, and
freeing me up to work without worrying too much about how
he's getting on. Matt has made some changes to the diner in the
last few years, but it mostly runs the same way it always has, and
I'm surprised how quickly my muscle memory kicks in. *It's like
I've never been away,* I think, as I wipe down the surfaces and
check the supply of cookies and cakes to make sure we aren't
running low on anything. I'm still turning Jennifer Gould's
comments over in my mind when another opinion reaches my
ears, again coming from Dad's table.

"It's the school, I'm telling you. What that woman has done
since she took control of it -"

"Oh come on, Simon. She might be a bit of a dictator but
that doesn't make her a murderer."

"Who are we talking about now?" I find an excuse to clean
the tables nearest to Dad so I can join in his conversation
with Simon O'Connell, another of Westhaven's gentlemen of
a certain age, hoping I might pick up some more insight into
the numerous controversies surrounding George Hamilton's
life and untimely death. I think back to the two women in
the pharmacy and am surprised that they aren't the only two
Westhaven residents angry about the new high school
principal.

"Principal Ayres." Simon bends over the table, carefully
rolling a cigarette. I clear my throat and he lifts his head,
offering me a sheepish smile. "Aw, I ain't gonna smoke it in here,
Ronnie. Just getting organized."

"What about Principal Ayres?" I ask, dismissing him with a wink. "I keep hearing about all these changes she's made to the high school. She asked George Hamilton to retire, didn't she?"

"Asked? Forced is more like it!" Simon hoots. "He'd still be there today if she hadn't escorted him off the premises herself. Made up some jumped-up reason they couldn't keep him on." He shrugs his shoulders. "So the guy was a bit of a dinosaur. Most of my teachers were when I was a kid. Didn't hurt me any." He moves from rolling cigarettes to counting change and I wonder if he's ever actually going to order anything, or just take advantage of my good nature to sit here shooting the breeze for free.

"Why the sudden interest in Westhaven High School?" Dad's watching me almost as intently as I'm watching Simon, and I see his eyes darken with suspicion. "Are you looking for a change of career?"

"Just curious," I say shortly, and retreat back towards the counter to greet the next customer I see approaching the diner. I'm not quick enough to avoid hearing Simon's question about what I do for a living and Dad's proud answer. I haven't told him I'm on borrowed time at my job, and I'll be lucky if I still have it by the end of the week. I'm still dodging my boss's calls and I know sooner or later she's going to stop trying and just send me my termination notice by email. And it's not her fault. I haven't exactly been a *present* employee lately, and there are peaks and troughs in our business, like in any other. If she has to let somebody go it's more likely to be me than anyone else. I don't want Dad to know that, though. He'll blame himself for keeping me here, away from the office, and the last thing I need is for him to derail his recovery by worrying about me. *Besides,*

I think, smiling as I neaten things up behind the cash register. *It's kind of fun working here at the diner again. Maybe I should be looking for a career change...*

"Well, isn't this a blast from the past!"

Melissa Barnes is beaming at me, holding out a ten-dollar bill as she orders a hibiscus tea with honey. It takes me a while to find that specific tea, and she takes great delight in informing me that Matt special-orders the blend, just for her.

"I'm the only person in Westhaven who drinks it!" She laughs, and I continue to rummage in cupboards until emerging triumphantly grasping the pink-patterned cardboard box. "You should try it," Melissa urges. "Very healthy." I take a sniff and grimace.

"Maybe next time." I add a scoop of fresh leaves to a pot and pour hot water over it, leaving it to steep for a minute while I ring up her order. It's funny how quickly *Ms. Barnes* has become *Melissa* in my mind, whereas George will stay *Mr. Hamilton* forever. Thinking of him makes me sigh, and my change in mood doesn't escape Melissa's notice.

"Something wrong, Veronica?"

I turn to smile at her, but that only makes her frown darken.

"You're thinking about George, aren't you?" She shakes her head, sadly. "Such a shame. He was one of the good ones. Of course, he didn't always think so highly of me!" She laughs, and from what I know of their differences I can well imagine what Mr. Hamilton had said to her over the years. "How's your dad doing?"

"Ask him yourself," I say, nodding to where Simon is finally getting to his feet and moving on with his day. "I brought him to the diner to keep an eye on him while I hold down the fort here and I think he's quite enjoying his local celebrity status." I hand Melissa her tea and watch as she tiptoes over to Dad's table, hesitating before joining him. In another minute, they're chattering away like old friends, and I happily go back to work, busying myself with cleaning up before my next customer comes in. I'm not sure what makes me glance back at the odd couple but when I do, Melissa is rummaging in her bag for something. She emerges a moment later, clutching an unmarked bottle of capsules she offers to Dad, who eyes them skeptically.

"What's in 'em?"

"Oh, all sorts of things to promote health and healing." She begins listing off the ingredients and one of them catches my ears. "Turmeric, black pepper, powdered cassia bark - that's cinnamon - "

"Did you give these to Mr. Hamilton?" I march over to take the bottle out of my Dad's hands and I hold them up to the light, squinting through the dark amber glass to make out a couple of dozen waxy-looking capsules. "Or something like them?"

"Certainly not!" Melissa says, coldly. I guess I spoke a little more sharply than I meant to. She snatches the bottle out of my hand and drops it back into her bag. "I just thought it might compliment your father's recovery. I wouldn't have risked giving them to George, not with his allergy." She sniffs. "Not that he would have accepted any of my *hippy herbal nonsense*, anyway."

"Right." My heart is jackhammering in my chest, but that soon gives way to guilt when I see the shadow on Melissa's face.

I've upset her. "I'm sorry," I say quickly, laying a conciliatory hand on her shoulder. "I didn't mean that to sound like an accusation."

"S'ok." She sniffs. "You aren't the first person to treat what I do with suspicion."

I remember the argument she had with TJ and wonder how often he's had cause to debate her remedies with her even before that day.

My thoughts are on my friend, again, but before I can ask Melissa if she's seen or spoken to him lately, the door to the diner flies open and Bella Villodan strolls in, stopping dead in the middle of the room as she spots me in my Slice of Life Diner apron.

"Veronica?" Her eyes narrow. "What are *you* doing here?"

"Helping out a friend," I say, then clarify which friend. "Matt, I mean. He asked me to cover for him while he goes to speak to Sheriff Foster." I force myself to smile. "What can I get you?"

"Oh, I don't know..." She trails off, looking as if she'd rather be anywhere but here if I'm in charge. I'm about to remind her that she's perfectly free to leave and come back later if she wants to, but then the door opens and another couple noisily enter.

"What a waste of time! I know he's just doing his job, but really! You'd think he might have made some progress by now. And the way he spoke to us!"

"It was an interrogation, babe, what did you expect?" I hear the smile in Matt's voice and am unsurprised to see it as he turns to greet me. "Hey, Ronnie. Everything go ok?"

"Just fine," I say, slipping out of the apron and handing it back to him, along with the keys I had clipped to the belt loop of my jeans. "And you?"

"It was ok."

"It was *not* ok!" Anna tosses her head and turns towards the friend who will offer the sort of comfort she feels she needs. "Bella! It was awful. Sheriff Foster acted as if Matt and I were criminals! Like we had anything to do with what happened to that poor, poor man."

"Of course you didn't!" Bella coos sympathetically. "It's a tragedy. A terrible, dreadful accident."

My dad mutters something that I'm pretty sure nobody catches but me - and even then only because I'm paying super close attention to every little cough and sigh he makes. I look at him and he's bent over his crossword again, slowly progressing through the clues. I wonder if he's aware he spoke his thoughts aloud, albeit under his breath.

A terrible, dreadful accident that's going to make your life a whole lot easier, sweetheart.

My gaze travels to Bella Villodan, who is still hovering around her friend, making a huge show of concern and mourning for a man I know she wasn't particularly fond of. *Perhaps Matt was wrong - there seem to be more people than ever who wanted Mr. Hamilton out of their hair for good. But does that mean one of them actually made it happen?*

Chapter Nine

After settling Dad back in at home - he won't admit to being tired out from the exertion of sitting at the Slice for a couple of hours, but I'm determined not to push things - I open up my laptop and plan to crank through my work emails for an hour, only...there aren't any. Well, that's not strictly true. There are precisely three concerning tasks that are resolved, or very close to being finished by other members of my team. I click through them in all of five minutes, and then I'm left refreshing an empty inbox until one new email finally drops onto my electronic mat. I click to open it almost before I register my boss's name as the sender and feel my stomach drop as I read the single line of content. *Please can we find time for a catch-up call at your earliest convenience*? This is it, the moment I knew was coming. *I'm getting fired.* Not because of misconduct, at least I can comfort myself with that much. My boss might be a piece of work but she is fair, most of the time. And she knows my work has been good. I've rarely taken time off before now, and I know this was short notice but even she must understand the nature of *family emergency*. But jobs have been drying up for a while, and there were rumors long before now about layoffs. And if I'm not there, in person, to fight for them to keep me...

Well, she can wait a bit for my reply, I think, too tired to worry about responding straight away. I'm in no great hurry to be told I'm no longer required. I'm sure she's annoyed about me dodging her calls, but that's a battle I don't have the energy to fight right now.

There's a knock at my door and I turn towards it, startled to see Dad standing there, gripping a steaming mug in each hand.

"Dad!" I leap out of my seat and take one of the drinks from him, then guide him carefully towards the bed. He sways a little, and I help him to sit down. "What are you doing?" I sound sterner than I mean to, and I try to soften my voice. "You aren't supposed to be overexerting yourself!"

"I can climb a flight of stairs, Ronnie. I'm old, I'm not dead."

"Not quite." I frown at him, and he looks satisfyingly sheepish.

"Well, maybe I'll sit and rest for a little bit. I was worried about you, working away up here on your own." He glances towards my closed laptop and then looks at me. "How is work, anyway?"

"Not great," I admit, angling my chair so I'm facing him before sinking into it. "I think I'm about to get fired."

"Why?" Dad is immediately outraged on my behalf and I'm touched by his paternal anger.

"Company downsizing, or restructuring, or whatever they decide to call it." I shrug my shoulders. "It's not anyone's fault. And if it wasn't me getting let go it'd be someone else."

"So let it be someone else. Why should you be the one to suffer?" He takes a sip of his drink. "Unless...well, that would mean you wouldn't have to hurry straight back to the city, wouldn't it?" His enthusiasm is endearing. "You could stick around here a little longer. I mean, if you wanted to."

"I wasn't going to be heading back any time soon," I remind him. "Not until you're properly back on your feet." I pause, risking a glance at my laptop. "I guess now I'll be free to stay in

Westhaven even longer, so you can look forward to lots more days of me fussing over you to come!"

Dad makes a loud groan, then winks at me so I know he's joking. We lapse into silence, and I find my gaze wandering around the room, my old bedroom that has sat practically unchanged for the last ten years. Dad follows my gaze and smiles.

"Is it weird being back in your old childhood bedroom?"

"Dad." I roll my eyes. "You make it sound like I haven't even been back to visit!"

"You haven't much." He shrugs his shoulders. "It's always, *Dad, come and see me in the city! There's so much to do! There are so many places I want to show you...*" He mimics a high-pitched voice that sounds nothing like mine and I lean across the bed to punch him lightly on the arm. "Hey!" He laughs, jumping back out of the way. "What happened to me being too frail and feeble to even walk up a flight of stairs? Since when does that leave me fair game for this sort of violence?"

"Since you started it," I retort, but obediently settle back into my chair and agree to keep my hands to myself. I hear him take a noisy sip of his drink and decide that this might be just the moment to mention something else that's been on my mind a lot lately. I just need to find the right way to bring the subject up...

"How did you find it being back at the Slice today? You're not too tired?"

"Nope." Dad takes a noisy sip of his drink. "But I will admit to having relished the chance to rest my eyes for a few minutes downstairs while you were up here working." He eyes me. "Or not working." His features relax into a grin. "How about you? Like old times for you, being there, wasn't it?"

"A bit," I admit, stifling a laugh before growing serious. It's now or never. "Dad, why didn't you tell me you sold the business?"

He doesn't answer straight away, but he does drop his gaze, which is all the proof I need to know what Matt told me is true.

"You signed your half over to Matt. When?"

"A while ago." Dad's voice is barely a whisper. "Matt told you, did he?"

"You should have told me!" I hear the shrill tone in my voice and again try to soften it. "Have things got so bad?"

"Not really." He shrugs, shifting his weight awkwardly on the bed. "They were, for a while there, but then when the sale went through I could settle what needed to be settled. Things have been just fine since then." He winces, recalling the handful of unpaid bills I'd brought to him in the hospital. "More or less."

"Right. And the gambling debts you were racking up with George Hamilton?"

"Gambling debts?" Dad jerks upright, shaking his head ferociously. "No, honey, it's not like that. It's just a friendly game or two of cards. We play for pennies. One week I win, one week someone else wins. This time it was George's turn." He frowns. "It's just a bit of fun. Nothing serious. Nothing you need to worry about."

"Right." At any other time, I might not have been so quick to believe this, but I can see how seriously my dad means it, and I decide to trust him. "Well, that's good," I say at last, thinking that whatever else I have to fret about on Dad's behalf, I'm glad I don't need to add *gambling problem* to the list. Another thought occurs to me, and I voice it while I'm still turning it over in my mind. "What about the other people who have a hand in that weekly game? Anyone else among them who might owe George Hamilton more than a few pennies?"

"Hmm?" Dad's distracted by a hangnail and I repeat the question.

"Is there anyone else in your poker circle who might have a reason to want George Hamilton dead?"

"What?" He laughs, then realizes I'm serious. "Ronnie! I don't make a habit of spending time with murderers." He shakes his head. "I know things are seedy and dangerous in the city, but this is Westhaven. Small town, dull, nothing ever happens. You remember Westhaven?"

I nod, but I'm not as reassured by my Dad's words as he intended me to be. *I remember Westhaven.* I remember the weekly scandals in and out of school, the trouble kids I knew used to get up to on the weekend, the things our old and ailing sheriff would just let slide for a quiet life. I wonder how much of that is still going on, now that the kids I went to school with are all grown up. Now that there's a new sheriff in town.

My phone buzzes noisily on the desk, making both of us jump, and I reach for it, assuming my boss is tired of waiting for me to reply to her email and is reaching out directly. *Again.* I plan to reject the call until I see the unrecognized number on the display and curiosity makes me slide my thumb over to accept it.

"Hello?"

"Ronnie! Oh, thank goodness."

"TJ?" I'm so relieved to finally hear my friend's voice that it takes me a moment to register that the number he's calling me from isn't *his* number. And even though I know it's TJ's voice, it doesn't sound like him. He's upset, and I swallow my hundred-and-one questions to ask him the only one that matters right now.

"What's wrong?"

· · · ·

"MS. SWAN."

I don't know why I'm surprised to see Sheriff Foster waiting to greet me as I hurry into the sheriff's station that afternoon, with my phone and wallet in hand. I've never really bailed anyone out before, and I'm not entirely sure how to go about it.

"I'm here to see TJ," I say, as brusquely as I dare. There's the slightest flicker in the sheriff's eyes and I'm not sure whether it's amusement or annoyance, but in case it's the latter I immediately soften my request. "Please."

"Of course." He shows me through to the holding cells and I see TJ sitting on a narrow bench with his head in his hands. He's not aware of our entrance, and it isn't until Sheriff Foster clears his throat that TJ jumps to attention. "You have a visitor."

"Ronnie!" TJ hurries to the front of the narrow cell and clutches the bars. I glance at the sheriff before crossing the room. He doesn't stop me, but he doesn't make any move to leave, either. He's watching us carefully, but I'm so concerned about my friend that at that moment I don't much care. "Thank you for coming."

"What happened? Are you ok?"

"I'm fine." TJ tries to smile, but that only emphasizes how pale and tired he looks. "They think I had something to do with George Hamilton's death. I didn't!" He clarifies quickly, then peers past me to where Sheriff Foster is still standing. "I swear I didn't!"

"As you keep saying." The sheriff's low drawl is unmoved, and I turn to look at him. "Why don't you ask your friend where we found him?" he asks, with a sad smile. "And then see if you can't understand why we had to bring him in for questioning."

I sense the sag in TJ's posture even before I turn back to look at him. At first, he won't meet my gaze.

"TJ?"

"It's not what it sounds like," he says, rubbing at some imaginary stain on one of his hands. "I mean, I was there, but not for the reasons they think."

"Where?" My stomach turns over. I think I can guess the answer, but I need to hear it from TJ's own lips before I'll believe it.

"In George Hamilton's house." He shakes his head. "I had to check...I mean, I just couldn't understand why...and it's not like anyone was there to let me in."

I hear the click of Sheriff Foster's steps as he crosses the narrow room and comes to join us.

"Your friend here decided breaking and entering was a better option."

"I didn't break anything!" TJ says, his head whipping back up. "George Hamilton's bathroom window is always wide open. Year round. Everyone in town knows that! Every kid who grew up here has climbed through it at one point or another."

"Is that so?" The sheriff looks at me and I hate the way I can feel my cheeks redden. "Interesting. And I was told Westhaven was a quiet beat. Never knew there was a whole town full of criminals living here."

"There isn't." I toss my head and focus my attention back on my friend. "So why were you so desperate to see inside George Hamilton's house?" TJ's gaze flickers to the sheriff and I wonder if this is the whole reason he asked me to come down here. This is the question he's wanted answered, and he knows TJ might actually tell me what he wouldn't have given up in an interrogation. There's a long moment where I can practically see TJ's mind whirring but in the end, I see him reach a decision. He pointedly turns away from the sheriff to look only at me.

"The epi-pens."

"What?"

I sense something imperceptible shift in Sheriff Foster's posture.

"There weren't any. Not in his kitchen, not in his bedroom, not in his bathroom. None." TJ shook his head. "Just like he didn't have one with him at the festival. He should have." His voice drops and I lean closer to hear it. "I've been filling his scripts for years. He should have had an epi-pen on him at all times with the severity of his allergy. He should have had spares at home. He just got a new one the other day. So where is it?"

I turn to the sheriff, determined to advocate for my friend the best I can. I may not be a lawyer, but I've certainly watched enough legal dramas to know that bluster works, sometimes, and I'm determined to use it now.

"You can let him go now. He's told you why he was there. He didn't commit a crime."

"He was in a house he shouldn't have access to."

"Come on. Like he said, all the kids in Westhaven have climbed through that window at some point in their lives."

"Even you?"

I look at TJ, who has sunk back on the narrow bench seat, looking like a shell of the man he's become. It's not the first time the sheriff of Westhaven has thrown him in lock-up to scare him, but our old sheriff, Wilbur Hart, was about as scary as a teddy bear. He gave kids more chances than was wise, in a lot of cases, but I know something he said or did must have been enough to knock some sense into TJ. He thought he'd left that life behind him. Being back here can't be healthy, especially not with this arrogant new sheriff throwing his weight around.

"He didn't hurt anyone," I insist. "And you can't tell me that point about the epi-pens isn't going to help you with your investigations."

"Is that right?" The sheriff rocks back on his heels, surveying me with amusement. I roll my eyes. If he wants me to do his job for him, then I will. Especially if it'll help get my friend out of a hole.

"Mr. Hamilton died of an allergic reaction, right? One that would have been reversed if he'd had his epi-pen on him. Which he should have had. Unless someone removed it." I raise my eyebrows. "Like maybe the person who dosed him with an allergen to begin with."

The sheriff takes my point and then glances at TJ. I shake my head. This is emphatically not the direction I wanted him to take this in.

"And as TJ said, if he'd just got a fresh batch they should have been in his house, if he did just forget it at home."

"Maybe your friend was there to collect them. Maybe he wanted us to think exactly what you're suggesting."

"And did you find them on him?"

Sheriff Foster shakes his head with a sigh. Even he knew that was a reach.

"Sheriff?"

We both turn as Deputy Dell bursts into the holding room clutching her phone. She's so excited she barely notices me as she bustles over to the sheriff, holding her phone out for him to look at.

"They got a print. A shoe print. On the window frame."

"Is that so?" Sheriff Foster squints at the screen, then looks at TJ. I can see his mind making the same connection as mine. TJ's shoes don't match that print. And they're about an inch too small. He draws in a slow breath and hands the phone back to his colleague. "Send me that, will you?" He turns back to me and smiles, but there's nothing warm about the expression. "Well, Ms. Swan, it looks like your friend can go home. For now."

I can't resist smiling back, and I load the gesture with all the *I told you so* energy I can.

"Maybe, while Deputy Dell here sorts out the paperwork, you can spare me a moment of your time to finally give us that statement you promised?"

My smile falters. I don't want to leave Dad alone - again - but something in Sheriff Foster's eyes suggests this is not the time to be anything less than fully cooperative.

"Sure," I say, stifling my resigned sigh. "I'm not sure I have anything to say that can help you, though."

"I don't know. You certainly managed to understand and explain the importance of Mr. Hamilton's missing epi-pens. Maybe there's something else you've noticed that my deputies have so far failed to."

Sheena Dell sucks in a breath of annoyance, but I don't think he meant to insult her. He's looking at me, and I can hear the cynicism dripping from his smooth voice.

Well, I didn't plan on being best buddies with the new sheriff of Westhaven but I certainly didn't want to make him my enemy. I guess it's too late now...

Chapter Ten

"**B**ella Villodan."

Sheriff Foster asks me outright who I think might be responsible for George Hamilton's death and Bella's is the first name that comes to mind. As soon as I say it, though, the idea starts to take shape and I begin to think I really might be onto something.

"Bella Villodan? Mr. Hamilton's next-door neighbor?"

The sheriff couldn't look more disbelieving if he tried, but then I remember he didn't grow up in Westhaven. He didn't know Bella in high school. *Murder is the very least of the things she's capable of.*

"They didn't like each other," I begin.

"Clearly a motive for murder."

The sheriff's lips quirk and I can see he's trying very hard not to laugh at me.

"It's more of a motive than TJ had," I shoot back, which he concedes with the slightest tilt of his head. "And then there's opportunity. She was right next to him when he died."

"That was Anna Chambers." He flips back through his notes to check, then looks at me. "An easy mistake to make, I suppose."

I try very hard not to lose my temper.

"Where Anna Chambers goes, Bella Villodan follows. They're like two sides of the same evil coin."

"Right. But if we're just fixing the blame on people who were right next to Mr. Hamilton when he died that doesn't exactly limit our options. There's Anna and Bella and Matt..."

I make the slightest intake of breath that betrays more than I mean it to. Sheriff Foster glances at me then looks back at his notes.

"Many of these people we've already cleared. And they were quite happy to wait around and talk to us right after the incident happened. There were only a couple of people desperate to break ranks and get away that day." He looks at me again and I shift uncomfortably in my chair.

"I had to collect my dad -"

"From the hospital. Yes, I remember." He looks up at me now, with something that might be concern. "How is he doing, your dad?"

"Recovering." I glance at the clock on the wall of the station. "I shouldn't leave him too long."

"I'll just keep you a few minutes more, don't worry." Sheriff flips his notebook to an empty page and looks up at me expectantly. "So you've given me your movements on the day, which confirms all the information we already had. Why not tell me why you think Bella Villodan is the criminal mastermind behind all this?"

I meet his gaze carefully, trying to determine whether he's teasing me or not. He waits, and in the end, I shrug my shoulders and decide to take him at his word.

"Like I said, they didn't get on. They were neighbors and they were having a long drawn-out feud about a tree, or a fence, or...some kind of boundary issue. I don't know all the details. But they were very angry with each other about it."

"Not uncommon among neighbors."

"Right. Well, now that Mr. Hamilton is dead, the issue goes away, doesn't it? Bella already has the landscapers in quoting her for the work she couldn't do when he was alive."

"Well, I guess that's a little insensitive -"

"She needed someone else to blame, right? And who better than a guy she's hated since high school?"

Sheriff Foster raises his eyebrows and I can tell this idea isn't settling with him.

"You think Bella is framing TJ to get even with him over some old high-school grudge? That's a bit extreme, isn't it?"

"You don't know Bella like I do."

"Clearly." He makes a note on his page, but I can see he thinks I'm delusional if I think my theory actually has legs.

"She likes to get her own way," I say. "And she hangs onto things. Slights, or old arguments. I'm kind of surprised she's even talking to me these days, after some of the rows we had back when..." I trail off, realizing too late that my own logic might just as easily be used to incriminate me now. *Maybe I'm trying to blame Bella to settle my own kind of grudge against her.* I draw in a breath. "I bet Bella was the one to call in and report TJ being in Mr. Hamilton's house. She probably watched him climb through the window, counted to ten, then dialed your number."

There's a long pause before he speaks again.

"Well, that's an interesting theory, Ms. Swan, but actually it wasn't either of the Villodans who called us about the break-in at Mr. Hamilton's. That was thanks to another neighbor. They have a video doorbell which happens to overlook that part of the street. So you don't need to drag up old grievances from a decade ago between Bella and TJ." He hesitates. "Or between you and her."

"You don't get it. People in this town hold grudges. And most people never leave, so the same friendship circles and issues just fester for years and years."

"You did."

"I did what?"

"Leave." He smiles humourlessly at me. "And then right when you came back, boom! There's a murder. And you certainly seem very eager to pin the blame on Bella Villodan, with the added advantage that it gets your boyfriend off the hook."

"TJ isn't my boyfriend," I answer too quickly, and pick the wrong point to object to. "And I didn't kill anyone! I liked Mr. Hamilton! We had coffee together just the other day. He's the one who prompted me to even enter the pie competition to begin with."

"I seem to recall hearing you were the winner. What did you bake?"

"A pumpkin pie." I swallow past the lump in my throat. "With cinnamon - but I labeled it very clearly, and I know Mr. Hamilton didn't eat a bite of it."

"Do you play cards, Ms. Swan?"

The non-sequitur catches me off-guard and I stumble to keep up. This is something of a skill he has and I think, despite myself, that he's probably very good at his job. *I don't know why on earth he's come to work here, in that case.* Westhaven might not be perfect but it's hardly the crime capital of the USA.

"What? No. Yes. I mean, I can, but I don't make a habit of it."

"Not like you father?"

"My dad was in the hospital," I begin, getting annoyed that this sheriff seems intent on messing with my head. "And Mr. Hamilton was a friend of his."

"A friend he owed money to."

"They played a regular hand of cards," I protest. "You're going to have to round up half the old guys in Westhaven if you're going to blame this on their poker game." I feel my cheeks flush and recall with embarrassment that this was the very accusation I leveled at Dad only a couple of hours ago. "They play for pennies," I say, reiterating what my dad told me. "And they tend to win and owe in regular rotation, from what I hear. That's hardly a motive for murder."

"Did your boyfriend - sorry, your friend TJ - tell you that he often joined those poker games? Or perhaps he played on a different night than your dad did. For a lot more than pennies."

My mouth opens and closes in stunned silence. I knew TJ played poker - he and other kids at school were constantly getting in trouble for playing on school grounds. Now that I think of it, they probably learned from Mr. Hamilton, who sometimes used less than sensible means of connecting with his students and building rapport with them.

"What do you think, Ms. Swan? Is *to make a debt go away* a more or less likely motive for murder than a neighborly squabble over a boundary fence?"

• • • •

"THANKS FOR GETTING me out of there."

TJ and I have been walking in silence for several minutes and it's not until we turn the corner and are out of sight of the sheriff's station that he tries to talk to me.

"You're welcome," I answer automatically. My mind is still turning over everything Sheriff Foster told me. It's a lot more than he should have, I reckon. My head aches and I press one hand against my temple. We talked in circles, and I'm sure I gave away more than I gleaned, but that still doesn't explain why he chose to tell me about TJ's poker playing - or the fact that his debt to Mr. Hamilton adds motive to any case the police might choose to build against him. He had to know I would ask TJ about it the first chance I get. Which is now.

"When were you going to tell me that you owed Mr. Hamilton money?"

"Hm?"

TJ turns to look at me, and I can tell from his face that Sheriff Foster wasn't exaggerating a word. He did owe money - and a fair amount of it.

"Poker games." I rub my forehead. "First Dad, now you. Who else played? Pastor Brook?"

"Only occasionally." TJ grins, then sees my expression and his smile slips. "Look, V, you may not have noticed but there's not a whole lot to do around here. Westhaven is a small town. Friday night poker games with the guys are a harmless way to blow off a little steam and hang out. So yeah, I play, and your dad plays, and half the guys in this town have joined for a hand or two from time to time." He jerks his head towards the diner as we pass it. "The evenings Matt hosts it are the best. We get fed into the bargain."

Matt too? My heart sinks.

"You know Sheriff Foster thinks that's your motive for killing him. He said you owed Mr. Hamilton a chunk of cash, and getting rid of him clears that debt pretty nicely."

TJ is already shaking his head before I even finish speaking.

"I don't believe him," I say, quickly. "But it's not going to hurt their case against you to have such a clear motive."

"Then he'll have to hold that against half of Westhaven." TJ clenches his teeth. "George Hamilton was a shark. He took money off almost everyone he played against. It's one of the things that got Erik's back up so much about that dumb fence."

"What?"

TJ shakes his head.

"You know, that ridiculous feud between George Hamilton and the Villodans. Erik used to get fired up about why George didn't just rip the fence down and replace it like they wanted. *It's not like he can't afford it*, he used to say. *Heck, Simon O'Connell would probably do the work for free to clear some of what he owed.*" He shrugs his shoulders. "I guess none of that matters now. They'll replace it themselves before the house is even on the market."

I nod, slowly turning this detail over in my head. Yes, it was true that Bella Villodan was miserable living next door to George Hamilton. It was true that she was angry about his behavior and she would certainly be happier now that he was out of her life, but she wasn't the only one who felt that way. And if Erik is the action-man I keep hearing he is, could he have taken it upon himself to find a solution? A *permanent* solution?

"I have to get home," I say, suddenly.

"Right, to your dad. Shoot, Ronnie, I'm sorry. I didn't mean to make you leave him for so long. I guess I should go home too." TJ stifles a yawn and I realize, for the second time, just how exhausted he looks. He's still on edge, though, and I wonder if he wants to be on his own right now.

"You know, I was going to cook dinner for Dad and me. Nothing fancy. Pasta, with some kind of sauce from a jar. And vegetables, much to Dad's delight." I smile, hoping the invitation seems more low-key than it feels. "Do you want to join us?"

Chapter Eleven

The evening feels almost festive when TJ agrees to join us, and not only does his presence lift my dad's spirits, but it even manages to distract me from the dismal day I've had. My job might be on the line, and there is a very possible murderer on the loose in Westhaven but for now, we have good food, good company, and good jokes.

"I found a book called How to Solve Fifty Percent of Your Problems."

Dad is so busy laughing that it takes him a minute to reach the inevitable punchline. "So I bought two!"

Well, maybe not good *jokes.* I stifle a groan and start to dish up, directing TJ to help carry the plates to the table. There aren't many problems that can't be improved with pasta. I give Dad a deliberately small portion of the dish, loading up his plate with greens to make up for it.

"Hey, this is pretty good!" TJ says, after taking a bite of his meal.

"You don't need to sound so surprised!"

"It's almost as good as Pamela Kaufman's pot roast!" Dad chimes in, taking a hearty mouthful. "Maybe we should add you to the Westhaven Women's League Mercy Meal Pantry."

"The what?" TJ laughs.

"I told you that wasn't a real thing!" I turn to him. "Pamela Kaufman has been round here practically every night since I came back dropping in casseroles and pot roasts and meals to make sure Dad is well taken care of. She claims it's part of some women's league initiative but I think Dad is the only person she cares about."

Dad opens his mouth to protest but I jump in quickly before he has the chance.

"You've got to admit it's strange, this interest she's taking in him. I mean, it's not exactly like we're right next door!"

"Where does she live?" TJ asks, making good inroads into his meal. "Maybe she just happens to pass this way a lot so you're on her mind."

"Unlikely," Dad says, reaching for a glass of water. "She lives on the other side of the high street. Out near the Villodans." He pauses to take a sip. "And George Hamilton."

"She lives where?"

I've never heard this before and now, all at once, I start to see the significance.

"Opposite George Hamilton's house. You must have known that, Ronnie! They've both had those houses for as long as anybody can remember. Back when Bill Kaufman was still around -"

"I just remembered something I have to do this evening," I announce, my words tripping over themselves in their eagerness to be spoken. I turn to TJ. "Would you mind staying here for a bit to keep an eye on Dad?"

"Hey!" Dad protests. "Dad is right here and can hear everything you're saying, you know."

"Dad also remembers he's only just out of the hospital and needs to accept a little bit of extra care now and again, doesn't he?" I blow him a kiss and he lets out a sigh but drops his protest.

"Sure, I can hang out for a bit," TJ says, with a wary look in my dad's direction. "If I'm honest, I could do with the company. Today wasn't the best day I've had lately."

"Oh?"

I kick TJ lightly under the table. I haven't explained to Dad about his arrest, or about my having to go and bail him out of the sheriff's station yet. My father may have mellowed where TJ is concerned now that we're all adults, but I don't think he needs any reminding of my old friend's chequered past. *And I don't want to give him anything else to worry about*, I think, conscious that if I confessed all to my dad about my current hunch about who killed George Hamilton he certainly wouldn't want me to run around Westhaven investigating it.

"I recorded the game for you the other night," I say to Dad. "Maybe you and TJ can watch it together." I meet his gaze and try to suggest he'd be doing me a favor by keeping an eye on TJ, rather than the other way around. This goes over a lot more easily than my first comment and I knock it over the line with one last suggestion. "And maybe I can swing by Lucky's on my way back and pick us all up some ice cream for dessert. Frozen yogurt for you, Dad, but even that's better than nothing, isn't it?"

I start stacking our empty dishes so I'm spared the sight of my Dad's eye-roll, and TJ jumps up to help me, following me into the kitchen.

"What's up?" he asks, as soon as the door swings closed behind us. "Where are you going?"

"Nowhere!" I try to sound bright and indifferent but am not particularly persuasive because TJ frowns. "I just...have to take these casserole dishes back to Pamela Kaufman." I see the clean dishes stacked on the sideboard and seize the excuse for my evening errand. I drop my voice to a confidential whisper. "I wasn't joking about her interest in Dad. I'm grateful for her help, of course, but that doesn't mean I want her as a stepmother. And I don't want to leave Dad again. Would you mind hanging out with him just until I get home?"

"Of course." TJ smiles, and I'm reminded of how close we once were. He holds my gaze just a moment too long and it might be the stress of the day weakening my usual defenses, or the nostalgia of this evening, or...

The doorbell rings and I jump. TJ moves and the air between us shifts and I'm left wondering if he felt what I did, or if I imagined the whole thing. *Probably just my imagination*, I think, acknowledging that it has been working on overdrive lately. *If I'm not trying to solve a murder, I'm making believe a romance where none ever existed before...*

"Are you going to get that?" TJ asks when the doorbell chimes a second time. "Or are you going to sneak out the back and leave me to deal with whoever it is?" He raises his eyebrows. "If Pamela Kaufman is here to stake her claim on your father, I'm not offering myself as a substitute."

I laugh as I head to the door, but I secretly wouldn't despair if it was Pamela - then I can ask her outright about who she saw sneaking into George Hamilton's house and when, and maybe resolve this whole thing before the evening is even over. I open the door and am surprised to find it's not Pamela at all, it's the last person I expected to see standing there.

"Matt?"

"Hey, Ronnie, I just wanted to -" He stops talking, seeing something over my shoulder that makes his earnest expression drop into a scowl. I turn, curious at what has caused such a change in my usually easy-going friend, and see TJ carrying the last of the dishes through to the kitchen from the dining room.

"What's he doing here?" Matt's voice is little more than a growl. He pushes past me into the house and winds up standing between me and TJ as he comes back from the kitchen. "You know he broke into George Hamilton's house this afternoon?"

TJ is on the defensive immediately. He glances from Matt to me and back again, then straightens to his full height, subconsciously squaring off against the new arrival.

"Oh, like you've never done that before, Matt? Every kid in Westhaven has climbed through that window before now."

"Right. Every kid. Not grown men."

I intervene and drag Matt back towards the door.

"It was a misunderstanding," I insist. "It's all cleared up now." That's not strictly true, but it's close enough, and I'm a little scared of how quickly Matt jumped to anger over TJ's actions and his very presence in my house. They were never close friends, but it wasn't like they ever had cause to dislike each other much. *Then again, Matt was pretty quick to suspect TJ of making a mistake with the pills he prescribed Mr. Hamilton when the murder first happened.* "TJ?" I call over my shoulder, keeping my gaze fixed on Matt. "Are you ok to stay here with Dad until I get back?"

"Sure thing." He's going out of his way to sound agreeable, and I get the impression he's grinning behind me to goad Matt. It seems to be working: my friend looks like he wants to punch something. A wall. *TJ's face.* I lay a light hand on Matt's arm. "I have an errand to run. Maybe you can come with me?"

Matt says nothing but he does obediently turn and march out of the door ahead of me. I shoot TJ an apologetic look, but he doesn't look as upset as I would be to have provoked such a reaction from easygoing Matt, and I wonder just how civil these two are to one another on a regular day. I don't make it far down the street before I get some idea.

"I can't believe you're still hanging out with TJ. After all these years you still haven't figured out he's a loser?"

"He's my friend," I say calmly. It's a little strange to me to see usually friendly Matt have such a decidedly unfriendly opinion about someone. Then I remember who he's spending all his time with and things start to make a lot more sense.

"You know the sheriff questioned him today about the murder?"

"The sheriff questioned you today," I remind him. "And your girlfriend. Where is Anna, by the way?"

"At the Villodans," Matt grumbles. "I'm on my way there, I just wanted to check in with you first. To see if you knew about - to see if you were ok. And to say thanks for watching the diner for me this afternoon." He smiles, and I see the black cloud lift just a little. "It was good to see your dad out and about. He's on the mend, then?"

"He is," I say. "Slowly. And if you're going to the Villondans' you can help me carry these." I dump one of Pamela Kaufman's casserole dishes into Matt's hands. "I need to return them to Pamela Kaufman and say thank you for all the meals she's been bringing us lately." *And ask if I can check her video doorbell footage*, I add silently, praying that Pamela will have captured the very evidence I need to prove my hunch, one way or the other. I need something to persuade Sheriff Foster of TJ's innocence because despite the rogue footprint I'm not convinced he's going to let my friend go without a fight. *Especially not if people like Matt and Anna are adding to his suspicions.*

"So you and Anna." I eye Matt. "How long has that been a thing?"

"A while," he admits. He doesn't meet my gaze and I fancy I see the faintest hint of a blush. *Good. He should be embarrassed to be dating such a monster.* But he doesn't seem embarrassed. He seems...happy. My stomach roils and I wonder if I ever knew Matt even half as well as I thought I did. He was like a big brother to me when we were kids, and I looked up to him and leaned on him when my Mom left, when Anna and Bella's mean girls act made high school a living hell, when I finally got my ticket out of Westhaven and into the rest of my life. That Matt is still here, but he's different somehow. *That'll be Anna's influence*, I think, wondering if we'll ever be as close again as we once were. It's unlikely, if he's decided the Annas and Bellas and Eriks of Westhaven are the kinds of people he wants to associate with.

"Do you guys spend a lot of time hanging out with Erik and Bella?" I try to keep my voice neutral but decide that this is another avenue for research I might as well exploit while I have it. Matt might know more than he realizes about Erik and Bella and their long drawn-out feud with George Hamilton.

"A bit." Matt looks my way, suspicion etched into his features. "Why?"

"Just making conversation." I hump the casserole dishes from one hip to the other and pick up my pace. "I don't want to make you late."

Matt frowns like he doesn't quite believe me, which is fine because I'm not exactly telling the truth. But I do want to get to Pamela quickly and find out whether my hunch is correct. *Because if it isn't, we're back to square one, and TJ is going to remain at the top of Sheriff Foster's list of suspects.*

"That's Mr. Hamilton's house, isn't it?" I point to the familiar building up ahead, silently assessing that the prim and perfectly kept lawn next to it must belong to Erik and Bella Villodan. I turn my head. "So this must be where Pamela Kaufman lives."

"This is the one." Matt opens an elegant wrought-iron gate and ushers me through it, glancing over his shoulder at his friends' house before following me with a sigh. I hesitate, ready to take the dish off him and send him on his way, but before I get the chance to, Pamela's doorbell buzzes and crackles and her familiar warm, welcoming voice pours through it.

"Veronica Swan, is that you, dear? And who's that with you? Oh, Matthew! Hold on just a minute you two, I'll be right there."

Matt is standing next to me, smiling rigidly into the camera on Pamela's digital doorbell, and he leans closer to me, whispering through clenched teeth.

"Some people shouldn't be allowed to use new technology. Do you think she spends her whole time peeping on the street and spying on all her neighbors?"

"Probably," I say, with a nervous flutter in my chest. *I'm kind of counting on it...*

Chapter Twelve

Stepping inside Pamela Kaufman's house is like stepping back in time. I know Matt feels it too, because he seems to shrink into himself, regressing ten or even twenty years to the same Matt I idolized throughout my childhood. I half expect him to ask permission to go on through to the backyard to retrieve a ball.

"So, what can I do for you kids this evening?" Her gaze focuses on me and she grows visibly concerned. "Veronica, is your father alright?" She notices the casserole dishes about the same time I remember we're still holding them.

"I wanted to bring these back to you," I say, swallowing the urge to add a *Ma'am* at the end of my sentence. "Dad's doing much better, thank you." I smile. "He says your food is certainly helping with his recovery."

"Really? He said that?" She blushes and I feel a momentary pang of guilt at putting words in my dad's mouth. Well, he didn't *not* say it.

"We're both very grateful for your care," I say, and mean it. I see now that Pamela Kaufman did go out of her way to ensure Dad and I had enough to eat, and there aren't many neighbors I can think of near my apartment in the city who would do half as much in the same situation.

"Where can I put these dishes, Mrs. Kaufman?" Matt asks, shifting into helpful-neighbor-kid mode and taking the one I'm holding to add to his. "In the kitchen?" He heads on through, then turns to me with a look that says *you wanted to talk to her, so talk!* He's right. I didn't come all this way just to be nice.

"Mrs. Kaufman."

"Pamela, dear!" She smoothes her house dress and smiles at me. "We've known each other long enough that I think we can be on first-name terms with one another now, don't you think?"

"Pamela." I return her smile, hoping that my next question isn't going to catch her too off-guard. "I couldn't help but notice your doorbell."

"My doorbell?" Mrs. Kaufman tilts her head to one side in confusion. "Oh, you mean my natty little spy camera!" Her eyes sparkle with mischief. "Yes, I'm rather pleased with it, I must say. I've never been one for technology. Resisted getting a cell phone for the longest time! But my nephew Charles told me about these doorbells where you can see who's at the door - for security, you know - and ever since my Leo died...well, you just never can be too careful, can you?" She looks at me and blushes. "I suppose you think it's all rather silly. I mean, this is Westhaven. It's not like where you live, in that big, bustling city. But..."

"I don't think it's silly," I say, quickly. "It's very sensible. I'm trying to persuade Dad to do the same." Another lie. "Maybe you can help me persuade him it's a good idea." I'm rambling now, trying desperately to get Mrs. Kaufman on my side before I ask her what I need to ask her. "I like how you have yours positioned, angled so it sees the whole street."

"Yes, dear. That's so I don't miss any deliveries or anything. And it helps me keep an eye on the neighbors." She seems to realize just what she's admitting to and hurries to clarify her words. "That is, to make sure they're ok. Of course, it didn't quite work out that way for poor George." She sighs. "Although..."

"That's what I wanted to ask you about. I was talking to Sheriff Foster earlier -"

"You were?" Pamela brightens, and I decide I've found yet another key to her heart in mentioning the name of the new sheriff. "He's ever such a nice young man, don't you think? Moved all this way from the south at the drop of a hat - and I can't think why, because as I understand it he'd had great success out there and was on track to really make something of himself in law enforcement. But, well, I suppose sometimes people just want a change, don't they, and I'm sure sleepy little Westhaven is about as different as it can get from what he's used to. You'll be feeling the same, I expect, although you haven't given up your big city life to move back here, it's just a visit. Not like Seth. What were you saying, dear? You wanted to ask me something?"

She changes topic so quickly that I'm thrown momentarily until I see Matt reappear from the kitchen. He's framed in the doorway and jerks his head towards the street.

"Your doorbell camera!" I blurt out. "I was told - Seth told me -" I cringe a little at invoking the sheriff's name as if that justifies my being here. Pamela seems to like him, though, so maybe if she thinks he's confided in me she will be more likely to do so, too. "Seth told me that your camera recorded TJ - that is, recorded *someone* breaking into George Hamilton's house today." I blink but hold Pamela's gaze. "I wonder if it might have picked up anything else, say, earlier this week?"

"Well, I don't know about that." Pamela frowns. Something in her demeanour shifts and I'm worried I've lost her. I decide to double down on the Sheriff Foster connection in hopes that might work in my favor.

"I told Seth - Sheriff Foster, I mean - that I was going to return your dishes tonight and that's when he mentioned you're living so close to Mr. Hamilton. I had no idea you were such near neighbors. It's such a devastating loss, you know, and I know the sheriff is working hard to bring whoever was responsible for his death to justice. We all want that, don't we?"

"I thought they already arrested somebody," Mrs. Kaufman prickles. "An old friend of yours, if I'm not mistaken."

Pamela Kaufman is not quite as easy to deceive as I thought, and I decide, at last, to opt for honesty.

"The sheriff did take TJ in for questioning today, but I don't think he had anything to do with what happened to George. Do you know there ought to have been medicine to stop George's allergic reaction? TJ filled his prescription. But he didn't have that medication on him, and when TJ -" I wince. "When he broke into George's bathroom, he couldn't find any evidence of those drugs at all. So I think - and Sheriff Foster agrees with me - that someone else got to them first. Maybe they used the same route TJ did. And maybe your camera recorded them, too." I hold my breath, looking as hopeful and innocent as I can. I don't trust myself to break Mrs. Kaufman's gaze, but I can sense Matt at the very edge of my peripheral vision. He's frowning, and I know he doesn't like how quick I am to do whatever it takes to help TJ out.

"Well, I hope you're right," Pamela says at last. "I mean, it's not nice to think of someone like TJ being involved in something like this. I used to go to him for all my prescriptions. Who knows what he might have been putting in my pill bottles!" She sighs. "Come on through to the kitchen. I have my laptop set up in there, and that's where the videos are stored."

I let out a sigh of relief and follow Pamela into the kitchen. Matt stands back to let us pass, then falls into line behind me, whispering something so low that it only reaches my ears.

"Sheriff Foster agrees with you?"

I shake my head. If I'm right about this, none of the white lies I just told will matter. And I really, really hope I'm right. Because if there's only video evidence of TJ climbing through George's window then, shoe print or no shoe print, it's going to be a lot harder to argue for his innocence.

"Here we are!"

Pamela's ancient laptop is propped up on the dining table, and after clicking a few things she brings up a view of the street, angling the screen so Matt and I can see it.

"This is right now. If I scroll backwards..." She hits a button and the video zooms up. I see Matt and me departing as we arrive, then disappearing backward down the street.

"This will be a few days ago," I remind her.

"Of course." Pamela frowns, then clicks out of the current view and into a folder with stored videos from the past week. "I don't keep everything on here," she says, with a nervous little laugh. "Just a few days' worth. You never know when it might come in useful." She clicks on one at random and I see from the date it's the day before the pie contest. The street is quiet, apart from the moment George Hamilton emerges from his front door, pausing to check his mailbox and then continuing down the street. My stomach turns over as I think that I'll never get to see him again, and then, not long after he disappears from view, someone else enters the shot. Someone who climbs up the side of George's house and into the bathroom window. The same route TJ took. *The same route every kid in Westhaven has taken at some time or another*. But this isn't a kid: it's a grown man, and it's one all of us recognize.

"Isn't that...?"

"Erik Villodan."

I can't fight the note of triumph in my voice. My hunch was right - and here's the proof. TJ is innocent! I lean closer, trying to tell from the blurry image whether the shoes Erik is wearing could possibly match the print Deputy Dell found.

"I can't believe it!" Pamela cries. "Then - oh dear! And I told Sheriff Foster that it must have been that nice TJ...Oh, dear!"

"It's fine, Mrs. Kaufman," I say, laying a hand on her shoulder and squeezing it encouragingly. "If you can report this to the sheriff as well I'm sure it will help them with their case. I know it will. Only, you must report it. Right away. Shall I come with you? We could go now?"

"Ronnie..." Matt is frowning as he looks at me, but before he can say another word, his phone rings. He glances at the screen, wincing at the caller ID, then answers, stepping a little away from us to take the call. "Hey, babe. What's up?"

"Could you email me a copy of this, Pamela?" I ask, scribbling down my email address on a nearby notepad. "Then we can take it into Sheriff Foster together. I do think the sooner the better. Or perhaps he will come out here?"

"No! Stay there. Look, I'll be right over."

Matt's voice sounds anxious and when I look at him his face is folded in a frown.

"What's wrong?"

"We have to go." He glares at me meaningfully, then turns to Pamela. "Mrs. Kaufman, you've been so kind and helpful. We can't thank you enough. And Ronnie is right. You need to report this to the sheriff straight away. But right now Veronica and I have to leave."

"Of course, dears." Pamela Kaufman is surprisingly understanding about Matt's sudden and unavoidable urge to flee. "There, Veronica! I've sent you the file, and I'll send another copy straight to the sheriff. I don't suppose I need to go there in person, do you think?"

"Call him!" I urge. "Call the station. I'm sure he'll come right out to see you."

"Oh, do you think so?" Mrs. Kaufman's hand goes to her hair, then to her house dress and she purses her lips. "Well, perhaps I'll just change into something a little more presentable, just in case."

"Good idea," I say, as Matt takes me by the arm and very nearly drags me out of the house. "Thanks again! For everything!"

As soon as we're out on the street I shrug off Matt's hold.

"What's the matter?"

"That was Anna," he says, nodding across the road to the Villodans' house. "Asking where I was. I couldn't exactly explain, could I? But if she's in there, and *he's* in there..." His lips turn down at even the vaguest mention of Erik Villodan, who, up until about five minutes ago, had been one of Matt's best and oldest friends. "Come on. We have to go in."

"We should wait for the sheriff," I protest.

"Sheriff Foster?" Matt mimics the nice-as-pie voice that I'd used with Pamela and rolls his eyes. "No. I can handle Erik. And if he is responsible for murder, I don't want to leave either of the others alone with him."

• • • •

"VERONICA!"

I've crossed paths with my old frenemies often enough since I've been back that you'd think I would be used to the level of disdain they each manage to put into saying my name - but I don't usually get to hear it in stereo.

"I ran into Ronnie on the way here. You don't mind if she joins us, do you?" Matt slings a companionable arm around me and ushers me through the front door into the Villodans' house. At first I think it's a shield - to protect me from the scorn of his friends - but then I realize it's just as much to keep me from ditching him and doing a runner. It isn't until the front door is firmly closed behind me that he eases his hold on me and turns to greet Anna with a kiss.

"Come on in, Veronica," Erik says. He's the first of the three to recover and welcomes me with a warmth that might have been endearing if I wasn't currently quite sure I was standing in the presence of a killer. "Can I get you something to drink?"

"Oh, just a water," I say, hurrying into the kitchen after him. I'll fill my glass straight from the faucet before I willingly accept anything from a suspected poisoner. I may not have a deadly cinnamon allergy but I'm not about to take any chances where Erik Villodan is concerned.

"Are you sure? We're kind of celebrating..." He beckons me back into the living room, passing an empty wine glass to his wife. "Aren't we?"

"We certainly are!" Bella beams at me in that irritatingly superior way she honed at thirteen. "We were just telling Anna about our plans for the backyard, now that..."

"Now that Mr. Hamilton isn't here to object?"

Silence falls so suddenly it's like something has sucked all the air out of the room. I take a noisy sip of my water and hope someone else will be the one to break it. Finally, Matt comes to my rescue.

"So come on, what are the plans? You'll get rid of the fence at last, I suppose?"

"Finally!" Bella groans. "I can't wait to see the eyesore torn down. We might even make a little on the deal. After all, there's nobody here to clarify exactly where the boundary line is..." She giggles and goes to refill her wine glass. I see Matt's face pale and hurry to distract the others before any of them notice.

"It's good to see you again, Anna. How did things go with the sheriff today?" *Was that only today?* I take another sip of my drink, realizing too late that she hasn't taken my words for the friendly inquiry I meant them to be. She's glaring at me, then forms her preternaturally red lips into a slow, cruel smile.

"Oh, it was just a formality for Matt and I, wasn't it, babe? But I hear someone else had a very interesting time at the sheriff's station today." She leans forward, never taking her eyes from mine. "Is it true that TJ was arrested?"

"I heard something like that," Erik mutters, bending to brush some imaginary lint off his jeans.

"He broke into George Hamilton's house. Like, they actually found him in there. Can you believe it? He climbed right in through the bathroom window."

My mouth is dry, even though I've drained my glass. Fortunately, this time Matt comes to my rescue.

"Well, we've all done that before. Right, Erik?" Erik flinches but soon recovers himself with an unconvincing laugh.

"I certainly haven't!" Anna cries, jabbing Matt in the side. "I didn't know you were practically a criminal!"

"Come on, all the kids got dared to climb through the window into Ham's House at some point or other."

"TJ isn't a kid, though," Anna protests. "He's a grown man. And so I have to wonder just what he was doing -"

"Oh!" I jump to my feet, almost before I'm aware of it. Everyone turns to look at me, and I fumble the first excuse I can think of. "I have to go to the bathroom."

Bella rolls her eyes, then points me down the hall. Neither she nor Anna even wait until I'm out of earshot before they start whispering about me. Ordinarily, that would annoy me, but tonight I'm just grateful they can stay distracting calling out my numerous personal failings and giving Matt and me a little more time to figure out what we should do next.

Once I'm in the bathroom I lock the door and start rummaging through cupboards for something - anything - that might be even the smallest bit incriminating. If TJ managed to walk out of the station despite video evidence then I'm quite convinced Erik will manage it too, unless I find something else irrefutable. *You idiot, Ronnie!* I think, when I've disordered every shelf there is and still turned up nothing more shocking than off-brand soap. *This is the guest bathroom. There isn't going to be anything here that Erik doesn't want to be found. He's more likely to leave it in his bathroom upstairs.* I turn the lock and then ease the door open, creeping into the hallway and pausing just long enough to ascertain that everyone is busy. I hear Anna's hushed tones berating Matt about bringing me tonight and spoiling their evening, and I roll my eyes at Bella's enthusiastic agreement. She always was very good at backing Anna up when she needed to. Still, it frees me up from scrutiny for a few more minutes, and I creep upstairs, feeling certain this is my one chance to find out the truth.

The first door I open leads to a prim and neat-as-a-pin guest room so I keep moving, finding first the main bathroom - a quick rummage turns up nothing of interest - and then the master bedroom. I'm about to discount this when I see a small plastic container poking out from under the bed. I reach for it, then jerk my hand back, instead working my phone free and trying to snap a picture. Before I manage, the phone goes off, ringing loudly in my hands. I yelp and drop it with a thud on the floor, just in time to realize that all the whispered conversations downstairs have ground to a halt. I scramble to my feet, grab hold of the epi-pen I've found, and hurry towards the door, but it opens before I can reach it and I see Erik Villodan standing there. He spots the pen along with my phone and his face pales.

"What are you doing?" His voice is hoarse.

"Finding proof that you killed George Hamilton."

"What?" He backs up, staring at me in shock and surprise and I take advantage of his distraction to push past him and into the hallway. I don't make it far. Bella has followed her husband and is standing halfway up the stairs, glaring at me.

"You put that there!" she hisses, her green eyes narrowed. She turns to Anna and Matt, who are both standing at the bottom of the stairs. "Right? You both see what she's doing! She's determined to get TJ out of trouble and she doesn't care who else she gets *into* it." She points a shaking finger at me. "I bet that doesn't even belong to George. Or if it does it's one of the ones TJ broke into his house to steal today." She shakes her head. "I can't believe you would stoop this low, Veronica. Planting evidence. Framing my husband for murder."

"She isn't, babe." Erik is standing behind me, and when I look at him I see a frail, broken shell of the man he used to be. He's caught, and he knows it.

"What?" Bella crumples, and I find myself lurching forward to catch her as she falls to her knees.

"I did it," Erik says, and it's like a weight lifts off his shoulders at the admission. "I killed George Hamilton."

Chapter Thirteen

"Ok, everybody out. I just need to speak to Erik."

When Sheriff Foster arrived at the Villodans' house he was more than a little surprised to find his murderer quietly sitting in the living room, ready and willing to tell his tale. It was Bella who caused the most trouble with getting to the truth. She had been crying steadily since Erik's admission, and every time he tried to speak to the sheriff she would interrupt, or qualify, or offer some alternative explanation to what Erik was saying. After a few of these interruptions, the sheriff evicted her from her own living room.

"Deputy Dell, take everyone else away, would you? But keep them close." He glances at me. "I'm going to want to speak to each of you before the evening is through."

Matt and Anna, between them, help the weeping Bella Villodan into a dining chair, then pull one up on either side of her for each of them to sit in. I'm left standing awkwardly a few feet away. I don't fit in this group, and I feel a bit stung that even Matt doesn't seem to notice me standing alone.

"I need to make a phone call," I say in an undertone to Deputy Dell, whose eyes are as big as saucers as she watches over us. "I need to check in with my dad. Can I step outside for a moment?"

She frowns, and I know she'd like nothing more than to keep all of us right where she can see us.

"I'll just stand in the yard," I promise, pointing to the backlit patio. "You'll be able to see me through this window." At last, she relents, but there's a sternness in her look that suggests I'd better not go far if I know what's good for me. I'd expected to have to fight to call anyone, so I'm not about to take my relative freedom for granted.

The first person I call isn't Dad, though. It's TJ. He answers on the second ring.

"Where are you? Is everything ok? I was debating whether I ought to come looking for you."

"How's Dad?" I ask, before answering.

"Dozing in his chair." I can hear the warmth in TJ's voice. "We played a hand or two of cards - no betting, don't worry." He hears the sharp intake of breath I'm not quick enough to silence. "And look, I can stay here as long as you need me to, but what's going on? You said you were just going to Pamela's to drop off those dishes but you've been gone for ages." His voice hardens. "Is Matt causing trouble?"

The irony of TJ asking if Matt is causing trouble isn't lost on me and any other evening it would be enough to make me laugh. Not tonight though. In hushed tones, I give TJ the briefest rundown I can of everything that's happened tonight - that we found some evidence that pointed to another culprit for Mr. Hamilton's death.

"I'm off the hook?"

"You will be," I say. "Although I expect the sheriff will still have plenty to say about you breaking into the empty house, whatever your motives might have been." I sigh. "You were an idiot over that."

"I know. But I just couldn't figure out what had happened to those epi-pens. There are always meant to be some in any first aid tent too, but they had gone missing at some point during the festivities."

"Sherrif Seth will get to the bottom of it." I feel a lot more confident about that now than I did earlier this week, or even earlier today. I hear a sharp rap on the window and turn to see Deputy Dell glaring at me from inside the kitchen. She beckons me to come inside. I guess my reprieve is over. Once I check Dad really is ok and confirm that TJ is happy to stay with him until I can get home again, I end the call. It's only then I remember my missed call from my boss. I tab over to my messages and see she's typed something.

We need to talk ASAP, she's written. I sigh, but the thought of being told I'm losing my job doesn't sting the way it used to. There's a lot that hits differently once you've stared down a murderer, I guess. I tap out a quick reply as I take the slowest walk back towards the house.

Caught up at home. Sorry. Will call tomorrow. It should satisfy her for at least a few more hours. I make my way to the door and open it, stepping inside at the very moment Sheriff Foster emerges from the living room.

"Ms. Swan." He looks past me into the yard. "Making a bid for freedom again?"

"Just stepping out to make a call." I risk a smile. "Even hardened criminals get one phone call, right?"

He quirks an eyebrow and I wonder if he remembers TJ's one phone call that afternoon. *This afternoon?* Exhaustion hits me and I make my way towards the table but the sheriff blocks my path.

"I wonder if we could speak for a moment before I talk to everyone else." He looks around the room, but apart from Deputy Dell, who is watching us closely, everyone else stays hunched over the table, trying and failing to comfort Bella.

I turn on my heel and head back out into the yard, prompting the deputy to squeak out a desperate *"Sir!"* which makes the sheriff turn to look at her.

"I'll just be a moment, Deputy. And you should be able to see us both if we stay here close to the house."

"No! Sheriff Foster. What about..." She jerks her head towards the living room and Seth's head lifts in understanding.

"Not to worry. Deputy Lister is taking Mr. Villodan into the station for processing. He'll record his full statement while we finish up here." He turns back to me. "Ms. Swan?"

The Southern Charm act is intriguing, even I have to admit that, but I still haven't forgotten the way this man baited me all week, blaming my friends and often me for a crime that had nothing to do with us. *A crime I actually managed to solve for him.*

"You did tell me there was another explanation for this," he admits, sliding his hat back onto his head as he pulls the door closed behind us. "I guess I should have believed you when you told me your friend TJ's motives were pure." His eyes widen as if even he can't believe he's just said that.

"Did Mrs. Kaufman call you?" I ask, trying to work out how much he knows. He nods.

"She was quite insistent about my coming out to see her, and I confess I was tempted." He pats his slim midsection. "That woman can sure make a pot roast." He glances slyly my way and I find myself smiling, despite everything. "But when she said it was about what happened to Mr. Hamilton I resigned myself to skipping dinner and coming to see what was the matter. That's when she showed me the footage and showed me a second piece that showed you and Matt heading over here, and him practically manhandling you through the door." He eyes me. "So I wanted to ask you, without your friends around. Is everything alright?"

"Oh!" I nod, surprised and a little touched by his concern. "Yes! Yes. Everything's fine." I hesitate and he tilts his head in that way he has, giving me time and space to think while he waits for me to say more. "They're Matt's friends. Well, Matt's girlfriend's friends." I shrug my shoulders. "They weren't exactly expecting me to join them this evening."

"Or to have you expose the murderer in their midst, I'm sure."

If I didn't know better, I'd think Sheriff Foster looked a little impressed. Then the light shifts, and his expression returns to neutral and I persuade myself I imagined the whole thing.

· · · ·

BY THE TIME I GET HOME it's late, and I slip into the house to see TJ slumped in one of the armchairs, my Dad in the other, with the TV on low running a sports game they're both sleeping through. I ease the remote out of TJ's hand, which is enough to make him stir, and he blinks sleepily up at me.

"All ok?"

I nod, then pause to check on Dad. He's snoring so I leave him where he is and tiptoe out into the kitchen. TJ follows me and is just shrugging into his jacket, ready to head out into the night.

"Thank you for staying with Dad," I say, surprised at the flood of gratitude I feel. "I know you didn't expect to be here all night."

"It's not like I had anywhere else to be," he says, stifling a yawn. "But I'll pay for it tomorrow."

"Are you at work?"

He nods, running a hand through his hair.

"Assuming word hasn't gotten around about my being accused of committing a crime."

"I expect once Pamela Kaufman is through discussing the case with all her nearest and dearest people will hardly even remember who you are, let alone that they ever thought you were involved."

"Did you think I was involved?"

TJ is looking at me closely as he asks this and I realize that for a moment there he must have felt like everyone in town had turned against him. I shake my head, glad I don't have to pretend.

"I never doubted you for a second."

He smiles, like he's genuinely touched to know that I was on his side.

"We've been through a lot together, you and me, haven't we?"

"This week?"

"This week." He nods. "And way back when we were at school. You were my best friend back then, you know. And life here hasn't been the same without you. I haven't been the same without you."

"You haven't, Mr. Responsible Pharmacist Guy." I tweak his collar and then realize just how close we're standing to one another. Our eyes meet and for a second I think about what it would be like to kiss him, but then my dad stirs in the next room, his level breathing disturbed by a cough, and then his thin voice calls out.

"Ronnie? That you, hon?"

I drop my head and step away from TJ, who grins at me.

"I'd better get out of here," he says, glancing at his watch. "See if I can't grab a couple of hours of proper sleep before I have to get up and moving for work."

"Are you at the hospital tomorrow? Or the pharmacy on Main Street?"

"Main Street." TJ grimaces. "I dread to think what a mess it's got in. Whenever they bring in someone to cover they always interfere with my set up..." He trails off, blushing as he catches my eye. "Anyway, that's where I'll be if you need anything."

"Excellent. Because I have a very crotchety patient who needs his pain meds filled. I'll call in to collect them around mid-morning?"

"Perfect."

TJ calls a low good night to my dad, then slips away into the night and I tiptoe back into the living room, helping Dad out of his chair and getting him ready for bed with a smile I can't quite hide.

"You were busy this evening," Dad says. "Do I want to know what happened?"

"I'm sure you'll find out, one way or another." I drop a kiss on his forehead. "But not tonight. Get some sleep and I'll fill you in on everything in the morning. I'm sure Pamela Kaufman will be more than happy to give you all the details I forget."

He sniffs but even in the low light I can see the faint hint of a blush on his weathered cheeks. *Dad and Pamela...well, I suppose she wouldn't be the worst person in the world for him to care about...*

Epilogue

It turns out that spending an hour or two sitting in a booth at the Slice of Life diner is an essential part of Dad's recovery, or so he tells me the next day, and I can't object to the thought of being around people again. Westhaven is buzzing with news of the case, and the diner is the prime place for discussing it.

"It hasn't been this busy here in years!" Dad remarks, as I bring our drinks over to the only empty table available. "Matt should make sure there's a murder every week!"

I gape at him, and he breaks into a sheepish smile.

"Too soon?"

"Too soon. And too public." Putting down our drinks I help him into his chair and sit down opposite him. "Now can I trust you to stay here for a minute and not get into any trouble while I go and pick up your next lot of pills from the pharmacy? TJ is working and I want to check in with him."

"Tell him to take a break and come join us," Dad says, taking a swift sip out of my coffee - the caffeinated, sugary one he absolutely should not be drinking - before I'm quick enough to grab it. He winks, then hands it over. "Or at least tell him I say hello."

"Will do." I try to catch Matt's eye but he's inundated with customers and in the end, it's another familiar face who comes to my rescue.

"Veronica! Do you have space for one more?" Melissa Barnes squeezes through the crowd of diner regulars and extras towards our table. "It's so busy here today! Has something happened?"

"Only my daughter helping to solve the crime of the century." Dad beams proudly at me.

"He's exaggerating." I lay a light hand on Melissa's arm. "And here, you can have my chair if you don't mind keeping an eye on Dad for a few minutes while I run a couple of errands."

"I'd be happy to." Melissa's eyes twinkle with mischief. "It sounds like you're the one with all the gossip, Edgar. Maybe you can fill me in while Veronica is busy?"

Dad leans back in his chair, taking in a deep breath before he launches into what I affectionately think of as *storyteller mode*.

"Well, it all began last night..."

Confident I'm leaving him in capable hands, I make my way slowly out of the diner and along the high street towards the pharmacy which, I'm pleased to see, is a lot less full of irritable people than the last time I was here. It's so empty that I begin to wonder if anyone is working there at all.

"Hello?" I call, as I approach the counter. TJ pops up from behind it, clutching armfuls of boxes of pills and looking frazzled.

"Hi." He disappears again, and I hear muffled cursing as he noisily pulls things on and off shelves. He emerges a moment later, free of boxes, and grins at me. "And what can I do for you this morning?"

"I just need a couple of things for Dad," I say, digging into the pocket of my jeans for the script I hadn't yet gotten filled. "But you can take your time. I left him telling the great murder tale to Melissa at the diner." I take a sip of my coffee. "So I have all morning before he even misses me."

TJ laughs and sets about making up my order. When he comes back, he's still wearing the ghost of a smile.

"Maybe I should stop by and listen. I still haven't heard the whole story myself." He looks at me. "Unless you want to give me the cliffs notes version?"

"We figured out who killed George Hamilton. Sheriff Foster arrested him and got a full confession." I shrug my shoulders. "You, my friend, are off the hook."

"Thanks to you."

"Thanks to Erik Villodan making a full confession."

"Which he never would have made if you hadn't pushed him to it." TJ hands over my paper bag of pills and looks serious for a moment. "I really am grateful, you know. If he hadn't admitted everything..."

"They would have figured it out eventually. Erik switched out some of Mr. Hamilton's regular pills with those herbal concoctions he'd gotten off Melissa. One of the ingredients she used was cinnamon. It was only a matter of time before he took the wrong one."

"But to steal George's epi-pens too..." TJ shakes his head.

"And the ones in the first aid tent," I recall what Sheriff Foster told me about the case and shiver. "He was so calculated. I think he wanted it to happen at the pie festival so everyone would just assume it was an accident. And maybe people would have done if you hadn't gone to look for the epi-pens in Mr. Hamilton's house. The fact that they were gone too was suspicious."

"Don't I know it?" TJ groans. "I almost ruined the reputation it's taken me years to build in this town. People had finally started to trust me, to look at me as some kind of success story. *Westhaven bad boy come good at last* kind of thing."

"You were never that much of a bad boy," I say, taking another sip of my coffee.

"I'm glad you think so." TJ rolls his eyes. "I got in my share of trouble, and that stuff sticks in a town like this one. Maybe I should have taken a leaf out of your book and got out while I still could."

My smile just about holds. I haven't told anyone yet that I will be sticking around in Westhaven a lot longer than I planned. I finally spoke to my manager this morning, and the conversation went a lot better than I expected it to, even though the result is still the same. A downturn in work means they need to lose some people. I think we were both surprised - and relieved - when I volunteered to be one of the losses.

I don't exactly know what the future holds for me, but I know I won't regret starting it back here.

"Is there anything else I can help you with this morning?" TJ asks, as he eyes his shelves. I know he's itching to get back to reorganizing and I certainly don't want to keep him from it.

"This is it," I say, hugging the paper bag close. "But if you decide to take a break, come find us at the Slice. Dad told me to invite you."

TJ gives me a mock salute, then waves me off and I make my way back to the diner, pausing as I pass the sheriff's station. Erik isn't in there, but I shiver all the same, thinking of how close he came to getting away with murder. Would he have let someone else take the blame for his crime?

"Ms. Swan."

I stiffen, then turn to greet the owner of that familiar drawl.

"Sheriff Foster." I take a sip of my coffee. "You can call me Veronica, you know. Most people do."

He smiles and then points toward the station.

"Were you just passing, or have you found another complicated crime to unravel?"

"No crime today." I salute him with my coffee. "Just coffee."

"Well, good. I was promised a nice quiet beat when I moved to Westhaven. I certainly wasn't prepared for murder." He arches an eyebrow. "Or perhaps things only liven up when you're in town. Remind me when you leave again?"

"Actually, I think I'm going to be sticking around."

"Really?"

Do I imagine it, or does his smile grow?

"For a while, anyway. I'm on something of a hiatus and Westhaven is as good a place as any while I figure out my next move."

"It sure is." He opens the door to the station and then pauses, turning to tip his hat in my direction. "You have a nice day now, Veronica."

I'm still smiling as I make my way back to the diner, and I peep in the window while I finish my coffee, unsurprised to see a crowd of chatty friends and neighbors circling my father, no doubt discussing the murder in great detail, and my specific role in it. I grimace, then decide to stay put outside for just a little bit longer.

"Are you coming or going? Or just blocking the path for fun?"

I shiver at the familiar words, the familiar voice and the intonation, but when I turn my head I'm not looking at a ghost but Matt, who smiles sadly at me.

"What do you think? Did I get the level of cantankerous old man right?"

"Pitch perfect," I say, turning back to look at the diner. "Is it strange to think of him not being around here anymore?"

Matt nods and I see he's stepped outside to water the plants that line the wide front windows.

"Fortunately, as the only decent diner in a several-mile radius, I have no shortage of regular customers. But I don't think any of them will quite take the place of George Hamilton."

"Do you reckon you've got space for one more?" When he frowns, I rush to explain myself. "One more regular customer." I lay my hand flat against my chest. "I'm going to be sticking around a lot longer than I planned. Like maybe...forever."

Matt's whole demeanor shifts in an instant. He drops his watering can and throws his arms around me and for a moment I forget about our disagreements and his girlfriend and all the things that came between us the last few days. For a moment I'm just glad I have my friend back. It's only for a moment, though, before a pointed cough makes us jump apart.

"Well, well, well! Don't you two look cozy?" Anna smiles stiffly at me. "I didn't realize I was going to have to keep an eye on you around Veronica, Matt!"

"Ha!" Matt laughs, then sheepishly takes a step towards his girlfriend, before putting his arm around her. "We were just celebrating. Veronica's decided to stay in Westhaven for good."

"Oh? That's wonderful." Anna could not sound less delighted by my news. She nudges Matt lightly in the side. "I guess we'll have to find room for one more, in that case."

"One more what?" I ask, certain Anna is about to recruit me to the women's league. I have uncomfortable flashbacks to our high school cheer squad and shake my head to clear it.

"Matt didn't mention it?" This time Anna's smile is genuine, confident, and proud. She turns to me and extends her left hand. "We're getting married. The wedding isn't happening for a couple of months - at Christmas, if you can believe it - but if you're going to be sticking around I suppose it's only right that you're there. After all, we want all our closest friends to come along and celebrate with us, don't we?" She looks up at Matt as she says this and I see him turn an uncomfortable shade of red, before wrangling control of himself again.

"That's right," he says. "We do." He looks at me. "You'll come, won't you?"

By some miracle, I manage to match their smiles with one of my own that must be at least partly convincing. It takes all my effort to sound happy with this impromptu invitation and I'm pleased that neither of them seem to notice my distress.

"Your wedding? I'd love to come."

• • • •

Return to Westhaven in the next Slice of Life Cozy Mystery[1]
Wed, Dead and Gingerbread[2]

---

1. *https://books2read.com/u/bxGeJe*

2. *https://books2read.com/u/bxGeJe*

About the Author

When Rachel Beattie[1] isn't writing stories, she's usually reading them - especially of the cozy mystery variety. A lifelong devotee of Agatha Christie, she loves putting ze little grey cells to work and is especially fond of anything that can make her laugh while she's collecting a clue or two.

· · · ·

She regularly shares updates, news and progress on stories she's writing for on Ream[2] – as well as a host of other bonuses. Become a free follower for more information.

---

1. https://reamstories.com/rachelbeattiewrites

2. https://reamstories.com/rachelbeattiewrites